CW01267246

Copyright © Matt Shaw 2015

Cover art copyright © Matt Shaw Publications
Published: February, 2016
Publisher: Matt Shaw Publications

The right of Matt Shaw to be identified as author of this Work has been asserted by him in accordance with the Copyright, Designs and Patents Act 1988.

All rights reserved.
This eBook is copyright material and must not be copied, reproduced, transferred, distributed, leased, licensed or publicly performed or used in any way except as specifically permitted in writing by the publishers, as allowed under the terms and conditions under which it was purchased or as strictly permitted by applicable copyright law. Any unauthorised distribution or use of this text may be a direct infringement of the author's and publisher's rights and those responsible may be liable in law accordingly.

For more information about the author, please visit www.mattshawpublications.co.uk

For more information about Matt Shaw, please visit
www.facebook.com/mattshawpublications

With thanks to

Nicola Woods

Christina Davis

Gary Royle

James Hedge

Alan Kleynenberg

Chad Ferguson

Carron Offer

Frank Meyers

Colleen Cassidy

and

Gina Jones

Mathew Fuller

Stacey Cox

ROTTING

LIVING

F*CKS

The sequel to Rotting Dead F*cks

MATT SHAW

It has been five years since the outbreak.

No one knows what caused it and - now - those who survive do not care.

Survival is their only concern.

The danger does not come from the Rotting Dead F*cks who have since become Rotten Dead F*cks - lying half-starved and weaker than ever.

The danger comes from the remaining survivors.

The surviving world has many a Ted - all of them desperate to be King in their own right.

INTRODUCTION

The World Today

A GLANCE AT HELL'S HOUSE

TODAY

A scream echoed through the house - causing all who heard it to stop what they were doing and turn in the direction of the source. A second scream - high pitched - followed. The living who heard it ran in the scream's direction to see what was happening; all of them grabbing various weapons that were close to hand. All of them expecting the worst, yet none of them caring. They were used to it now.

The dead themselves, pushed against the bars of their cages - unable to proceed further despite the hunger driving them to find and eat the source of the noise. Undead groans of frustration scratching from the backs of their throats. Rows and rows of the undead, caged like the animals that they were.

A third scream.

With most of the house members now standing in the hallway, they could tell that it was coming from the third floor. They were used to screams coming from that particular floor but not screams of pain but - rather - screams of pleasure.

'Who's up there?' the latest house member to join the gathering group asked. He looked up the twisted staircase, climbing through the central part of the house, towards the third floor - a baseball bat with nails driven into the tip, gripped firmly in his hand.

'Gary,' a second man - closest to the stairs - said without looking back.

'Gary?'

'Gary Royle?'

'I don't know him.'

'He's new. Been here less than two days.'

A fourth scream echoed down the stairwell from the third floor. This time it didn't stop though. Gary - the man supposedly responsible - just continued to scream and scream, clearly in distress.

'Less than two days and he's on the third floor? Someone went through the rules, right?'

'Supposedly.'

'What the fuck is going on?!' another voice from down the hallway. Frank Meyers, the owner of the house. Or rather the *new* owner of the house. The original Master of the House was out the rear - his head blown out at the back by a hollow-point bullet when he refused to let Frank seek refuge within his country mansion.

The group turned and looked in Frank's direction. He was staggering down the far hallway with a bottle of whiskey in his hand. Both he and the bottle were half-drunk.

'What the fuck is going on?!' he called out over the constant screaming once more.

'New guy. Gary Royle.'

Frank reached the hallway. 'You all just standing here - not one of you cunts thought it a good idea to go up and see what the fuck his problem is?'

They shrugged. The man who had recognized that the screams belonged to Gary spoke out, 'You know what they say - they're screaming like that, they're already dead.'

'And what cunt said that?'

'You did.'

Frank looked at him. 'Get up those stairs and silence that cunt before I feel inclined to silence you.'

The man - clearly nervous - looked at the rest of the group, 'Someone come and give me a hand…'

No one moved and it was clear from Frank's face, he wasn't about to force them. Frank nodded towards the stairs - a gesture suggesting the man should quit being a pussy and get on with sorting Gary out, one way or another. The man - downtrodden - turned towards the stairs and started up them. Frank - meanwhile - turned to the rest of the group.

'I let all you cunts stay here… First sign of trouble and you all freeze like little girls. You realise that one day, you might actually have to get your fucking hands dirty, right? I provide you entertainment, I give you fucks a safe roof over your heads, I oversee that we're all fed and watered and that we have power and… What do you cunts do for me other than cost me resources?'

No one answered. No one dared to. They knew better than to do so when Frank was drinking - or had been drinking. He was dangerous sober. He was lethal drunk. And - currently - he was halfway between drunk and sober and so his reaction could go either way.

Without another word, he downed the remnants of the whiskey and bottled the closest of the group directly in the face. That was the way it was going to go then… 'You need to learn how to be more grateful!' he shouted, over and over again whilst stamping his foot down on the bleeding house member.

The rest of the group, slowly backed away.

*

James Hedge, the man foolish enough to speak out to Frank, was standing on the second floor. His eyes were fixed on the stairs leading up to the third floor, wondering what he was going to find when he got there. Gary was still screaming - clearly in both pain and distress. James knew that was better though. All the time he was screaming, he hadn't turned into one of *them*.

What the hell was he going to see when he got there?

'And you - you're a fucking cunt as well… Clean this mess up,' Frank's voice boomed up from the ground floor as he instructed whoever to fix the mess he had just made. Whatever was happening up on the third floor, it had to be better than what was happening down there James decided. He gripped his golf-club tighter and pushed on up the stairs.

The third floor was a series of bedrooms. Most of the furniture had been trashed due to the fact that it wasn't required. Some of it destroyed for the sake of it and some of it broken down into firewood. The beds remained though and that's where they… The scream became even more desperate as James reached the third floor landing, echoing down the hallway, from behind the third door on the left. The room which had been booked out for an hour.

James hesitated a moment. A loud thump from behind the closed door as something heavy hit the floor. James raised the club and cautiously walked down the narrow landing with his hands trembling - causing the golf club to visibly vibrate. He hadn't killed anyone before. He hadn't killed the living and neither had he killed the dead. He preferred helping people.

Can you even kill the dead?

Correction: He hadn't put them out of their misery.

He reached the door and tentatively put his hand on the handle. A few deep breaths and he twisted it, pushing the door open just as soon as the latch permitted. Immediately he stepped back, shocked by what he saw.

Gary was rolling around the floor, screaming. His trousers and pants around his ankles, all twisted up in a bunch. His hands were covering his privates. Legs and hands - all flesh on show - covered in blood and gore.

'Help me!' he yelled when he saw James standing there - a look of alarm on his face. 'She fucking bit me!'

On the bed was his date for the hour. One of the undead lying there with her hands cut off so that she couldn't scratch if she had managed to free her arms from where they were tied to the bed-head. The ball-gag that all workers were forced to wear - for the protection of the client - had been removed against the rules of the house. She was chewing something fleshy; a mashed up mixture of pink and red and a hungry look in her clouded eyes.

'What the fuck happened?' James asked, the golf club raised - ready to strike whatever came in his direction. It was a rhetorical question. It was obvious what had happened. Gary'd gone up for an hour - a reward for doing a good deed for the house (whatever that may have been) and he must have gotten carried away and removed the gag in the hope of - given the fact his cock was missing - some head. The fucking idiot. The dead don't suck. They bite. The first rule was - do not remove the ball-gag under any circumstances. Do not untie their arms from the bed-post. Fuck them, by all means, but don't fuck with them.

'Help me!' he yelled out again - clearly in pain.

James shut his eyes and - without a second thought - brought the club down on Gary's head. He raised it again and brought it crashing down for a second, a third and a fourth time. The first hit silenced the scream and sprayed blood across the room - splattering the wall in red, the tenth hit opened the skull.

When you're bitten, there are no cures. James liked helping people get better but sometimes you just had to know when you were defeated. This was one of those occasions and just because the appendage had been bitten off... The victim was still going to change. That was the way it worked. James did what he had to do and he didn't stop with ten hits. Twenty-three heavy hits with the club was what it took to mash the brain up - the only known cure for turning into one of *them*.

James slumped down on the floor, exhausted and emotionally drained. His first kill of what would be two for the day. He tried to think of it differently; he hadn't killed someone but rather - he had saved a house full of friends who could have been in danger when Gary changed. The worker's content groaning coming from behind him - mixed in with the squelching sound as she continued chewing the flesh - reminded him that she was there and also had to be dealt with. He knew he couldn't leave her alive. Not now she had had the taste of flesh. She would need to be put down just as Gary had been.

James pulled himself to his feet, using the golf-club as an aid to help him up. He knew there was no sense putting it off. It needed to be done so best just get on with it. With club in hand, he walked over to the bed. What made it worse was that it was his favourite girl. Most of them had become loose at the time of death when all muscles relaxed but she - Honey he called her - she'd remained tight.

He sighed as he raised the club back up in the air. It would take less hits to get to the mushy brain this time. The skulls of the dead were easier to crack. He closed his eyes and smashed the club down….

Just another day in paradise.

James sat down on the end of the bed with his back to the dead girl. He wiped some blood from his forehead, where it was slowly trickling down, unsure whether it was from him or from her. For all he knew it could have been from the pair of them. He glanced back over his shoulder towards the girl. She was naked, her legs slightly apart and the gash he'd fucked on so many occasions was staring directly back at him - almost winking at him, hinting that she was good for one more ride. He sighed again, she was such a great fuck and now she was gone, leaving the loose lasses behind in her wake.

Why the fuck had that idiot wanted her mouth when he could have had that? It didn't make sense. He ruined it for everyone.

James reached back with his free hand and pushed the worker's legs shut.

Such a waste.

The door burst open and James' friend - another medic - came into the room with a look of excitement on her face. Her name was Nicola Woods and - before finding the house - the pair had never laid eyes on each other before. Within days they'd managed to strike up a friendship, helped by the fact that - when the world was "normal" – they had both worked in the medical profession.

The way she burst in startled James, 'Scared the crap out of me,' he laughed.

'There's a cure,' she said - unable to contain her excitement.

'What?'

'There's a fucking cure!' she repeated. She stopped a moment when she noticed the carnage sprayed and squashed around the room, 'What the hell happened?'

CHAPTER ONE

MATHEW and STACEY

TWO TODAYS AGO

Mathew remembered the man standing by the side of the road - frantically waving at them and clearly distressed. He remembered his friend - Stacey - insisting that they stop to see if they could help the man with whatever his problem was. In this case, it looked as though the car he had been traveling in had broken down.

Mathew also remembered telling Stacey that it was a bad idea to pull over for the stranger. He had said that the world was not as friendly as it used to be - and she should have known that from what they had seen on their travels already.

Of course - Stacey being Stacey - asked how Mathew would have felt had it been him stranded at the side of the road trying to get help and the only car he had seen - possibly for days - drove straight on by without a care in the world.

She gave him the *look* too. The one which made him feel small and insignificant and hinted that it wasn't worth arguing with her if he wanted a peaceful life. Needless to say, he slowed down to a stop and - just as he had predicted - it had been a trap.

Now - having woken up with what he thought was a mild concussion - he was sitting opposite her, the pair of them strapped to the walls with heavy chains, and was now giving her the look. A look which said "I told you so" without having to actually say the words. She wasn't paying any attention to him. She could see what he was doing out of the corner of her eye and she wasn't going to give him the satisfaction.

'I told you so,' he said.

'Just don't even go there…'

Mathew cricked his neck with a satisfying crack. God only knows what they had hit him with but - whatever it was - it felt as though it had nearly broken a bone. He tried to rub his neck with his hand but the chains - keeping him attached to the wall – prevented him from reaching.

'Are you okay?' Stacey asked - suddenly consumed with guilt. She knew it was her fault but - there was little point in stressing over that now. Not now they had more pressing things to worry about; such as how to get out of this mess.

'What do you think?' He sighed heavily and changed the subject, 'Tell me, do you know where we are?'

She shook her head, 'They put a bag over our heads?'

'My head too? They worried I was going to recognise where we were whilst being unconscious? They say anything? You know - like what they want?'

'Nothing. Just told me to shut up when I tried talking to them.'

Mathew started tugging at the metal restraint around his wrist; a hope that either they or the brackets holding the other end of the chain to the wall would give.

'I've tried that,' Stacey said.

She may well have done but just because she couldn't free herself, it didn't mean Mathew couldn't either except... He actually couldn't. Pulling at the chains did nothing but bruise his wrists, breaking the skin on his left wrist slightly.

'Shit.'

Mathew didn't take his eyes from his sore wrist. He knew she was looking at him and she knew she was about to say…

'I told you so,' she said.

Mathew looked at her - irritated, 'You realise this is your fault, right?'

'How's that?' she asked.

He couldn't believe she couldn't see it, 'I was fully prepared to drive on by. I was happy to leave the guy at the side of the road. You've seen the films I've seen - when has it ever ended well when someone has stopped to help someone? Even in romantic comedies something goes wrong, even if it's just the car breaking down and the couple find themselves stuck out in the middle of nowhere.'

There was a moment's pause before she asked, 'Watch a lot of romantic comedies?'

'My wife likes them,' he said. He went quiet before correcting himself, 'Liked them.'

Stacey didn't say anything and the pair of them fell into an uncomfortable silence. Strangers might have thought differently, seeing them together, but they weren't husband and wife. They were both married but their partners - like so many other partners - were gone. Missing and presumed dead.

'I'm sorry,' Stacey said eventually, breaking the silence. She wasn't apologising for reminding Mathew of his wife. She was apologising for getting them in this situation. It was her fault and he was right to point it out but - now wasn't the time for the blame game. They needed to think about how best to get out of there. Or - at the very least - try and figure out where the hell they were.

Mathew didn't respond. It was clear from his face that he was lost in memories gone by. Stacey said sorry again - louder this time - breaking him from his thoughts.

'Do you have any idea where we are?' he asked. He didn't want an apology. He wanted out of the chains and - without knowing where they were or why they were there, it made it that little bit more difficult to figure a way out. He continued, 'I mean - I know you had a bag on your head but... Were we on the road for long? Any sounds you recognised? Anything that might give a clue as to our location?'

She shook her head.

'And they didn't say anything?'

Again, she shook her head before pointing out, 'They were talking... They just didn't say anything of note.'

Mathew was getting frustrated. It was bad enough he had allowed himself to be sucker-punched in the first place – even when he had suspected it was a trap - but for Stacey to have no clue as to where they were, or why they were there… He just wanted answers. In his mind the same question was going over and over again and again: Who the hell takes hostages in this day and age? Money was useless. If you wanted something you just took it. There was no benefit in taking someone hostage. The way he could see it, there was nothing to gain. He could have understood it had they simply stolen their car from them when they pulled over. That would have made sense. After all, there are many vehicles left by the side of roads or parked up in driveways but very few of them work or have fuel in. The car…?

'What happened to the car?' he asked Stacey hoping she at least had the answer to that.

Slowly - feeling stupid - she shook her head, 'They put a bag over my head. I don't know.'

He couldn't believe it. 'They wouldn't have left it there. Not a working car.' It was too valuable, even though the car itself would have been considered a piece of shit when the world was functioning properly. 'They must have had someone drive it back.'

'I'm sorry. I just don't know.' She paused a moment, 'Everything will be alright,' she said quietly. Mathew looked at her - unsure whether she was reassuring him or seeking reassurance herself. Mathew looked at the chains keeping him tethered to the wall. He wasn't sure how everything would be okay and he wasn't the only one questioning his future. Gina was worried too and for good reason - not that she looked worried from her outward appearance.

CHAPTER TWO

GINA

Gina screamed out and rattled the chains against the wall. She knew they were out there, beyond the closed doors and she knew they could hear her. She whipped the chains back against the wall again in the knowledge it would have been annoying the assholes outside. True enough, the door opened and Frank stepped in with a lady on his arm; Christina Davis.

'That's quite enough out of you thank you,' Frank said - a stern tone in his voice. The banging and senseless screaming had been going on for nearly an hour now and had given him a bitch of a headache, not that he'd admit it to Gina. He wouldn't want her having the satisfaction of causing him any discomfort. Besides, Gina had gone quiet the moment he stepped in - mainly because, the last time she had been in this position, and continued to scream, he'd beaten her without first undoing the restraints. Had he undone them, it would have given her the chance to at least try and defend herself from the flurry of punches. It didn't stop her from staring at him with a look of pure hatred though.

'Where should I put it?' Christina asked the question of Frank. She was asking about the tray she carried in her hands. A plastic knife and fork, a plastic cup of water and a paper plate with a bloody steak on it - Gina's reward for a good fight earlier that night.

Frank nodded towards the floor, next to where Gina was huddled up against the wall. He continued addressing Gina, 'You fought well today. What's that - nine in a row? One more to go…' Gina snatched the bloody steak from the plate as soon as Christina set the tray down; a swift movement which startled Christina, making her jump back. Frank laughed. He was used to the speed with which Gina moved and knew to expect a sudden reaction from her - part of the reason he stayed a few feet back. He turned to Christina, 'Hard to believe she was a vegetarian when we first started, huh?'

Christina didn't say anything. She just stood there, a look of horror on her face, and watched as Gina ripped the steak apart with her teeth, swallowing down large chunks of flesh as though it were her first meal since being half-starved.

'Look at you now,' James had turned his attention back to Gina.

She grunted between mouthfuls. Looking at her now she looked as though she were one of them - one of the undead. There was hate in her eyes without a trace of humanity. Her face was caked in blood - some of which was her own and some of which belonged to *them* and here she was - ripping flesh apart with nothing but her teeth. She looked a far cry from the woman she used to be; a wife of eleven years to Aaron, a mother to nine year old Ben and 4 year old Ruby, an owner of a cat called Tito, a sister to six brothers and sister. That woman was dead. The woman who used to work as a supervisor of a Factory Shop in St. Clears was gone with ninety percent of the rest of the popular - her family included - and what was left was one step away from animal.

'One more and you're free to go,' Frank continued. 'Back to doing whatever the fuck it was you were doing in the first place...'

What she had been doing - before finding herself in this building - was looking for fellow survivors; a society that she could try and become a part of. What she found though... This house and *him*. Frank smiled at her, curious about what she was thinking behind that cold, dead stare.

As it turned out, she was thinking quite a lot behind the cold, dead stare. She was worried about her family - even though she had the uneasy feeling they were dead - and she was stressed about all the stuff she had done to get where she was today; one away from being released.

'The good news,' Frank continued, 'is that we have two more recruits as of about half an hour ago. A male and a female. We're just letting them get used to their surroundings before we explain to them what is going on and then - well - then the game is on.' He smiled at Gina.

Frank was the one who made the rules up. He was the one who had told Gina she needed to survive ten fights in order to go home again. Gina realised, though, that it also meant he was the one who could change the rules too and the closer she got to the tenth round, the more she realised she wasn't ever leaving this house.

'You should feel proud,' Frank was still talking, 'you're the only one to have made it this far. You've certainly surprised all of us. Pissed off a fair few too, given that - at the start - most were betting against you. I mean, what are you? Five foot nothing? Vicious,' he laughed, 'truly vicious.' He nodded, as though agreeing with himself, and finished, 'Get some sleep and stop slamming those chains against the wall.' He didn't say anything else. He about turned and left the room with Christina in tow.

As soon as the door slammed shut, Gina started slamming the chains back against the wall until she was too exhausted to continue doing so.

* * * * *

It was rare for sleep to come to such an extent that Gina could dream, not that she minded. Her dreams tended to replay the life she used to live - before this - as opposed to what was happening now; a cruel reminder that things will never be the same again. No more nights watching *American Horror Story*, no more having a laugh with co-workers Michelle, Carol, Big Phil or Sam... Or even with her manager Nyrene. No more snugging down on a cold night with her Kindle in hand - reading her favourite horror authors. That life was gone in all but dreams.

Gina woke with a start; a short dream in which she was just sitting there with her Kindle in hand. There was nothing more to it; a simplistic dream which - under normal circumstances - wouldn't have even been remembered when she woke. Yet now - it stayed with her throughout the whole day, in the forefront of her mind - always there - along with the faces of the people she had killed. The people who were just like her.

Damn this house.

Gina's heart skipped a beat when the door suddenly opened. Christina stepped in, cautiously checking over her shoulder to ensure no one was watching her. She closed the door, quietly and backed-up against the wall furthest from where Gina was chained. For a moment, the pair of them just stood there in silence.

For a moment.

Christina was the first to crack, 'I'm sorry for what they've done to you.' She waited for Gina to say something but she didn't. She didn't even blink; just stayed there, huddled against the wall with her eyes fixed on Christina. 'If I could get you out of here, I would…' she said carefully. Christina was one of the lucky ones. She was allowed to live in the house - with the other home mates - without having to go through the ordeal forced upon Gina, and some of the other guests.

'You can get me out of here?' Gina pounced on the words spoken, the first time she'd properly acknowledged something someone had said since being in the house.

'I can't.' She explained, 'I thought this house was the chance for a new start, you know?' Christina started to cry. 'Four days. That's how long I've been here. I saw the lights on as I came up over the hill and - with nowhere else to go - I thought I would try the door.' She wiped her cheek with the back of her hand. 'I thought everything was fine to begin with. James seemed like a nice enough man. He was kind, he was welcoming… He said I was safe and then… I noticed things weren't as they seemed. He didn't let me go upstairs, then he started saying I had to work to pay my way - which is why I bring you your food - it's one of my tasks…'

'Get me out of these fucking chains,' Gina hissed.

'I want to, I do, but…'

'Get me out of these fucking chains,' Gina repeated herself through gritted teeth.

'He'll kill me.'

'You think he won't kill you anyway? One false move or when he gets bored…'

It was obvious from Christina's face that she did want to free Gina. She was just scared of the repercussions if it all went wrong.

'If I do - will you take me with you?' Christina asked. 'You've proven that you're strong. You're a survivor… I don't have the skills you have… I don't have…'

'Skills? They're not skills…'

'The way you killed those people…'

'They're not skills. I just don't want to die. I didn't have a choice. It was them or me and I want to live. I need to live. I need to try and find my family to see if they're still alive. I need…' she went quiet as she realised she was starting to get emotional. Since the first fight, she'd learned not to let the emotions show. James - and some of the other people living in the house - seemed to get a kick out of seeing the emotions. Give them nothing, that's what she wanted to do. Give them nothing.

'Whatever you want to call them… I… I can't do what you did… Please… If I can get you out of here - will you take me with you?' Christina pleaded once more, desperate to get out of the house. Gina didn't answer her. She didn't want to take this woman with her but - at the same time - she knew she couldn't get out of there by herself. Not unless she won the next fight and James was true to his word.

'He's planning your event for tomorrow night,' Christina said. 'They've already started taking bets upon whether you'll win or not. If you let me go with you - I can get you out of here tonight. You won't have to fight again. Yeah?'

Gina knew she didn't really have a choice but to agree although - in her head - she was already planning on how best to double-cross Christina. Without trying to show the clearly terrified woman her true intentions, the moment she was free - Gina planned to snap her neck like a twig.

'You get me out of here then,' she said quietly - almost reluctantly.

'And I can go with you?'

Gina nodded, 'You get me out of here and I will set you free.'

Christina smiled, unaware of Gina's play on words; she won't just be setting her free from the house but from this so called existence too. 'I'll get the key later, when he's had a little more to drink. I help you, you help me.'

CHAPTER THREE

THE HOUSE THAT HELL BUILT

6 MONTHS AGO

Classical music filled the grand rooms of the country mansion. The owners uncaring if any of the undead could hear from beyond the thick walls. The world was over. Help wasn't coming. No one knew what was happening out there, or why it had happened and it had gotten to the stage where fewer and fewer people cared whether they survived or not. Hope had long since died and joy was close to following too - seeing as every hobby you could imagine had, suddenly, become too risky to carry out for fear of attracting, or stumbling, into the hordes of the undead. Music was all Alan Kleynenberg had left to enjoy and - with that in mind - he played it as loud as his sound system would allow; consequences be damned.

It was the midnight hour and Alan was sitting in the armchair of his favourite room in the house - the living room. Up against one wall was the entertainment system - now powered by a generator - and across the other side of the room there was a pool table with a game half-played. Tucked up in the corner was his drinks cabinet which - as seen by the pessimistic Alan - was now half-empty; one full bottle of Scotch by his side ready for the seal to be broken no sooner had he finished his current glass - killing off the last bottle.

The vinyl record stopped playing the music as the needle reached its final groove. A gentle buzz from the speakers as the record continue to spin-on regardless of having nothing left to say. Alan tutted to himself, downed the last of his current glass, and stood up to flip-sides. As he walked across the room - to where the player was - he stopped suddenly and turned to the living room door. From out there, in the hallway, there was a knock-knock knocking. He frowned to himself as he wondered who - or what - was causing it.

Knock, Knock, Knock, Knock.

Pause.

Knock, Knock, Knock...

It was too precise and spaced out for it to be one of the undead. They didn't knock. They ran their long nails down the doorframe, clawing to come in.

Knock, Knock, Knock...

He had to answer it. If it was someone out there, they'd soon presume the property was empty and would come in anyway. The last thing he wanted was for someone to break a window, or a door, to gain entry as it meant the security of the building was compromised. As it stood now, with strong doors and small window panes - it was pretty secure and Alan wanted it to remain so.

Setting the now empty glass down on the side of the armchair, Alan walked out of the living room and followed the knocking noise to the main atrium. Another series of loud, purposeful knocks and it was clear - someone was at the front door.

'Who is it?' Alan called through the thick door.

'Hello?' a voice from the other side.

Alan repeated his question, 'Who is it?' he asked again.

'My name is Frank,' the voice called through. 'My friends and I were walking through the woods - looking for somewhere to rest up and we noticed your lights on...' the voice continued. Alan already knew where the stranger was heading and sure enough, 'We wondered if we could rest up for the night?' It was a fair request given that the night was the most dangerous time to travel - not because it made the undead any faster on their feet but because it made them harder to spot amongst the dark shadows - especially in the surrounding woodlands.

'I'm sorry but I don't know you...' Alan started with the excuses.

'My name is Frank,' the man said once more. 'Please - you'll really be saving us. We've already lost one of our own to one of the dead.' He pleaded again, 'Please... We will die out here.' It wasn't a melodramatic statement. At night the odds of dying increased by approximately sixty-five percent. But even so...

'I'm sorry - I can't let you in,' Alan said through the door - a strong, stern tone of voice hoping they'd take the hint and leave him in peace.

Before the end of the world happened, if someone had come knocking at his door, he probably would have answered it but not now. To those outside, it might have seemed harsh but the simple truth of the matter was - he trusted the living less than the undead. With the rotting ones, their intentions were clear from the start; they wanted to eat your brains and devour your guts for desserts. With the living… They pretended to be your friend and then - when you thought they were - they turned on you. Which was exactly what happened to Alan's wife. It hadn't been the dead that had taken her life. It was the living.

'Please - if you just look through the spy-hole - you'll see that we're good, honest people like yourself…'

Despite his better judgement, Alan peered through the spy-hole.

The gunshot rung through the air as the back of Alan's head opened up scattering brain matter over the floor behind him. The force of the shot - coming from the other side of the door - sent him crashing backwards against the far wall in a crumpled heap, his left foot spasming uncontrollably from nerve damage.

From the other side of the door - laughter was heard first followed by a heavy banging against the sturdy door, as each of the group outside took it in turn to throw their weight against it in the hope of breaking through.

* * * * *

Frank had been travelling alone but by the time he got into the house, his group was fifteen strong - made up of people he'd met along the way. People who followed him, without question, after he promised the ultimate sanctuary. Sanctuary he'd remembered back from when he had worked as a delivery driver for one of the main courier companies.

'Would you look at the size of this place,' he said - stepping into the mansion for the first time, after the door gave way thanks to the shoulder of Dave - one of the larger of the group. He had often seen the building from the doorstep, getting Alan to sign for his wares, but this was the first time he had seen the other side of it and - it was fair to say - he was suitably impressed.

Three stories in total with God knows how many bedrooms. A large staircase in the main atrium leading from the ground floor all the way up to the third level.

'Where the fuck are you going?' he suddenly called out to a couple of the group members who'd made a bee-line for the stairs.

'Going to choose our bedroom!' one of them called back.

'I don't fucking think so. First of all - I get dibs. This is my house now, cunt. Second of all… We need to plan the layout of the house. I have big plans for this place,' he said. The two men - apologetic - came back down to where Frank was standing. 'Listening to you fuckers, as we were walking through the woods - you lot think life is over and we're all just biding our time until we're dead but… Nope… This house here… This is our new start. This is how we start to live again, not survive but fucking live…' Frank couldn't help but smile as his mind started formulating his plan for the future. Like some of the other group members, there had been a time when he thought everything was over and that's when he had remembered this house and the safety he thought it offered out here - away from everyone else… Away from the undead. 'This house is going to be my Kingdom,' he said quietly. His words didn't go unheard but no one chose to argue with him. This was - after all - his plan and had it not been for his actions, none of them would be standing there now.

'So what is the plan now?' one of the group members asked. His name was James.

'I don't know about you guys,' Frank said, 'but I could murder a fucking drink. So - now we find where this dead cunt keeps his booze.' He smiled again and even gave a little *whoop* as he headed off down the first hallway, to investigate the many rooms.

'And then what?' James called out down the hallway after Frank.

'And then we start recruiting!'

CHAPTER FOUR

MATHEW AND STACEY

EARLIER

TODAY

The door to the room holding Mathew and Stacey opened and Frank stepped in flanked by a couple of his acquaintances, Nicola Woods and Chad Ferguson. Nicola was medically trained and insisted on checking over the new arrivals to ensure they hadn't been bitten - risking the house to an unplanned outbreak. Chad was just nosy as wanted to see whether the girl was worthy of a fuck - before *and* after they'd turned.

Mathew and Stacey had turned to Frank the moment he stepped in. No one said anything for a while. Stacey and Mathew were sitting there, waiting for him to say what the fuck was going on and he was just standing there, looking at them - smiling - trying to decide which of them would go first. Fairness dictates it should be the woman - Stacey - but she didn't look as strong as Gina and if Gina won the next round then he would have to let her go and - well - that couldn't happen despite the initial promise made. Frank lets her go and he knew there was a good chance she would come back for both revenge and the house. He couldn't allow that.

'Let us the fuck out of here,' Mathew suddenly hissed.

Frank looked at him and raised an eyebrow. Usually they begged to be released or they started to cry - sometimes both. They didn't tend to start off so aggressive. That usually came later. Frank turned his attention back to Stacey. Such a pretty thing. She would be a good addition to the third floor; a quick snap of her neck and - soon enough - she'd come back as one of *them*. Dress her up in one of the outfits stolen from the town's sex shop and - yes - she'd go down a right treat. And then, he turned back to Mathew, that would leave him for Gina and there's no chance she'd win *that* round.

Frank smiled again; it was all starting to come together.

'Did you have a nice night's sleep?' Frank asked. 'We thought about trying to get some mattresses down here, you know, to try and make it more comfortable for the new arrivals but -

truth be told - we need all the beds we can get. Thirty-three of us in here now and... Well, the doors are always open to new guests that we deem suitable for our requirements.' He repeated himself, 'Need all the beds we can get.'

'What the fuck is this?' Mathew pulled at the restraints. 'Why are we here? What the *fuck* is going on?'

Frank turned to Stacey, 'Is he always such a mouthy cunt?'

'Fuck you!' Stacey spat.

Frank laughed, 'See how you two are friends!' And - just like that - the smile faded from his face. 'You want to know what this place is?' he asked. 'You want to know what you're doing here? Well... Let me tell you...' He paused a moment - enjoying having his new houseguests hang on his every word.

'We need to get this done so I can check them over,' Nicola said.

Frank hissed, 'Relax! They're showing no symptoms. They're fine.'

'Even so...'

Frank turned to her - a stern look on his face, 'I said they're fine. Shut the fuck up.' He turned back to Stacey and Mathew, 'Sorry about that. Where was I?'

'I think you were pretending to be all important,' Mathew said sarcastically. 'Just tell us what you want and let us the fuck out of these chains.'

'If you don't stop talking to me like that, I'm going to cut your tongue out. I am going to cut it right the fuck out. And then... I'm going to cook it up and I'm going to fucking eat it. You understand me?' Frank paused a moment and let his sudden temper simmer back down. 'Where was I?' he said quietly - a rhetorical question. 'Ah yes.' He turned back to Stacey and Mathew, 'You two are the entertainment. See - a few of the residents like to gamble. I mean, obviously, we don't use money or anything like that. We gamble cigarettes, drugs… You know - rations which are getting harder to source. And, well, they gamble on deadbeat fucks like you in what I like to call *Fight Club*.'

'Wait a minute,' Mathew said suddenly.

Frank smiled. He half-expected Mathew to start begging for their freedom now he knew what was on the line. 'Something wrong?' Frank asked.

'The first rule of Fight Club is… You can't talk about…' Before Mathew finished his witty line, a reference from a film of the same name, Frank stepped forward and punched him square in the face forcing Mathew's head to violently turn and a splattering of blood to spill from his mouth.

'You two are going to fight. The only way out of this is to win ten fights…' Frank continued, 'You win ten fights and you get to go back to whatever shitty life you led out there before we came across you…'

'I don't think we should fight this one,' Chad said - licking his lips - as he eyed up Stacey, imagining all the ways he could use her body to make himself cum. He preferred his girls to not have make-up made out of bruises.

Without turning to look at him, Frank said, 'Don't worry - her… Form has been noted.'

'You don't understand, we can't be here… We have to get up North.' Stacey said quickly.

'Up North? What the fuck is up North for you other than rain?'

'There's an institute up there… It's government run… It's where they're looking for the cure…'

'It's true,' Nicola confirmed.

'You don't look like government bodies,' Frank said with his eyes fixed on Mathew. Frank imagined most government workers to be fairly straight laced in their appearance - clean shaven and tidy haircuts. Admittedly it had got harder to look after your appearance since the world went to shit but - even so - Mathew sported a mohawk. Not a haircut Frank imagined from someone with an important job.

'We're not,' Stacey continued with Mathew letting her do the talking.

'Then what the fuck business do you have going to their offices? You hoping they're going to get you out of the country? Let you on a private plane to some secure island somewhere? Good luck with that. They'll most likely shoot you on sight…'

'Don't tell him anymore,' Mathew said. 'Fuck him and fuck everyone else here.'

Mathew's sudden outburst was enough to raise Frank's curiosity and he silenced him with a swift kick to the gut and a 'Shut the fuck up.' Frank turned his attention to the other side of the room where Stacey was trussed up against the wall, 'You… Start talking.' Stacey didn't say anything much to Frank's frustration. He sighed heavily and reached behind him, pulling a large knife from between belt and jeans. He stepped back and leaned down placing the blade of the weapon against Mathew's neck. 'You need to start talking. Like - fucking - now. Or else I'm going to cut your cunt friend's throat and leave him to bleed out. Then - from other there - you're going to get to watch him turn when we lock you in here again. In fact, I might - just might - undo his restraints when he is dead. I'm sure it won't be long before he figures out how to pull away from the wall by which time he'll be able to merrily feast upon you.' He waited a moment before raising an eyebrow, 'So what is it to be?'

'Don't tell him. He won't believe you anyway,' Mathew said, even with the knife against his throat. His words were met with more pressure being applied to the neck from the blade. 'Fuck you,' he hissed again.

'You know - in a minute, whether she talks or not… I'm going to just fucking kill you for the fun of it.'

Chad laughed. His eyes still undressing Stacey. His imagination still in overdrive as to what he'd do to her as soon as he got the green light.

'He's been bitten!' Stacey said suddenly and loudly.

The room fell silent.

* * * * *

ONE WEEK AGO

Stacey looked at Mathew as though he were insane. She didn't move from her place, sitting at the far side of the living room they'd been holed-up in for the last month. She was surrounded by various empty packets of food; the last of which had been opened the night previous. These packets being the last this particular house had to offer them.

'We can't stay here. Resources are gone,' Mathew said.

'I get that, I do.'

'So it's agreed then.'

'I'm not arguing about that,' Stacey said.

'Then what's the problem? You're looking at me like I've shat in your favourite handbag.'

'I was fine with the whole plan, right up until the point you told me to bite you. That is why I'm looking at you like you've lost the plot.'

'You think?'

Stacey nodded, 'I'm sure. I mean, what is all of that about?'

Mathew lifted his top, revealing his bare stomach. He turned to his side a little, 'Just lean down and bite…'

'On your side?'

'Yes.' He looked her dead in the eye, 'But make sure it's hard. I mean - you need to pierce the skin. Trust me.'

'I don't want to bite you… What the Hell?'

'What if I told you it could save our lives?'

'I'd say you really need to start talking sense soon. What the Hell are you talking about?'

Mathew laughed. Perhaps he should have explained his plan before just telling his long-term friend to bite him. Still - looking at her face now - he was having too much fun winding her up; something which didn't get to happen as much anymore. The sense of humour and fun, despite their best intentions, was the one of the first things to die when the world started to rot. As fun as it was though, he was being semi-serious; he needed her to bite him. And - before that could happen - he'd have to explain why.

'Come on,' he continued, 'just think of it as a little love bite - with teeth.'

* * * * *

Nicola was inspecting the bite on Mathew's side. Frank watched on, waiting for her to give the verdict as to whether it was human or not. Chad was still watching Stacey, something she was now conscious of. He winked at her and she frowned back before breaking the uncomfortable eye contact.

'It's definitely a human bite,' Nicola said, pulling Mathew's top back down.

'Then how hasn't he changed yet?' Frank asked.

Nicola asked Stacey, 'When did this happen?'

Stacey shrugged, 'About a week ago.'

'The average person turns in three days. We know that,' Nicola said to Frank. 'If he was bitten by one of them, and it was a week ago… He should have turned.'

Stacey explained, 'We're going North because,' nodding towards Mathew, 'he's the cure.'

INTERVAL

REBECCA and CHRIS

<u>HOPE</u>

Rebecca was being difficult on purpose.

'I didn't buy it,' she said. A pedantic comment for the sake of being pedantic and Chris, Rebecca's husband, knew it. She didn't buy it because the concept of money no longer existed in this world. There was no money involved when you popped to the shops, there were no shopkeepers standing guard over their merchandise, there were no price-changes beamed down via a clueless head-office and - in some cases - there wasn't even any stock in the stores that hadn't been burned down. The world had gone to shit and it meant that - if you frequented a shop - you could ransack it for whatever you chose, not that much stock remained on the shelves these days; a fact which was becoming a very real problem for Rebecca and Chris.

'Okay, smart-arse, where did you get it?' Chris reworded his question with his eyes still firmly fixed on the crossbow in Rebecca's hands. She was sitting by the previously boarded window of their small two up, two down terraced house. The wood, once used to block the window, was in pieces on the floor next to where she was sitting on the old dining room chair.

'Ssh, you're putting me off.'

Chris stepped behind his wife and followed the crossbow's line of sight. If she was aiming for the rotten dead fuck at the far end of the street, she was too far to the left. If she was aiming for the one closer, and heading towards their building, she was too far to the right.

'You're going to miss. Whatever it is you're trying to hit, you're going to miss.'

'Fuck off.'

Chris noticed Rebecca had taken her glasses off for the shot. No doubt she had to in order to get her head closer to the sights for a better look. Even so - when you're sight isn't the best to start off with - it's probably better to keep your eye-wear on, 'You'll find it easier if you…'

'Fuck off,' she muttered again as she continued trying to control her breathing. Slow and steady. Concentrate. Think about the target you want to hit. Study their movements. Watch the pattern with which they move or - in this case - lurch. And then - when you're ready - take a deep breath and gently squeeze the trigger. Don't just press it. You need to be gentle. Controlled. Not that it took a lot to fire an arrow from this particular weapon with its hair trigger.

The hair trigger, the weight of the crossbow, the way it comfortably sat against you when you pressed it into your shoulder - God only knows what something like this would have cost when money was a currency. God? God's as dead as the fuckers lurching their way towards the house. Dead pricks had followed Rebecca back from the shopping run. She was slower on the way back, pushing the shopping trolley, but they were always slower. You'd think it was a saving grace - the fact that they were slow - but it wasn't because you knew, no matter how slow they were, they never stopped. They kept on coming and eventually, when you stopped for a quick rest, they'd catch up with you. That is, unless you…

She took a breath and…

'I'm telling you you're…'

She squeezed the trigger and the bolt shot from the front of the crossbow and flew up the street where it bounced off one of the many abandoned cars. The shrill screech of the car alarm pierced the near-still air.

'Fuck!' Rebecca turned to Chris, 'Thanks for that!'

'How was that my fault?'

'You put me off and you know you did!' Rebecca got up from the chair and propped the wooden board back up against the open window. 'You realise they'll be banging on the door to come in soon?'

'Then we will deal with them then - just as we have every other time we've been followed back'

'*We?*'

Chris hadn't gone out for a few months now. Not since he had hurt his leg falling down some stairs in one of the shopping malls. He had blamed the fact that it was one of those awkward staircases where there were gaps between the steps but it was obvious that alcohol was to blame. When Rebecca had found him, crumpled at the bottom of the stairs, he had stunk of the cheap booze he'd found on the floor amongst the debris of smashed bottles and display units. To this day he denied being drunk but she knew. They both did. Whatever the reason was though - his leg still hadn't healed properly and he now walked with a limp as he hobbled around; a huge disadvantage when out and about shopping for supplies whilst trying to outrun the walking dead - which is why Rebecca now completed the supply runs by herself.

Rebecca started moving the newly acquired shopping from the bedroom doorway to its new home in the bedroom; the one room that had been set up as their den. They had the rest of the house free to do with as they pleased but it had been a mutual decision to only live in the one room upstairs. Not only was it easier to defend but it also gave them more time to climb from the window to get away should anyone get in through the front or rear door.

Clothes had been tossed in the corner of the room and the shelves that once kept them neat were now used for cans of food and bottles of water. The underwear drawer had been emptied and was where the candles were kept. Everything in the room had changed to how it used to be. Even the television - useless since the power died along with most of the population - had been thrown down the stairs as "just another" obstacle an intruder would need to clamber over in order to get up to Chris and Rebecca.

Chris picked the crossbow up and loaded a bolt into the front of it. He primed it before setting the weapon back down and removing the board from the window space once more. Picking the crossbow back up, he looked down the sights towards one of the closer zombies.

The sight magnified it slightly giving him a better look. The skin was pasty and hanging off in dead clumps, the lips were pealed back from the mouth revealing teeth tainted with whatever poor son of a bitch had fallen before it. Its eyes were unblinking and misted over with grey. Its hair clung to its scalp in greasy lumps. The clothes were tatty and ripped in various places with the shoes faring worse thanks to the way they were being dragged repeatedly across the hard concrete. The hands were stuck in what appeared to be a claw-like position - as though desperately clutching to something unseen. It really was an...

'Ugly son of a bitch,' Chris muttered.

As Rebecca put the last of the supplies away, Chris took a shot. The bolt shot past the target's rotten head and dug into the unflinching gut of the one close behind. Rebecca snorted at his attempt.

'Fucking sight is off,' Chris mumbled. He turned to his cocky wife, 'Least I hit something.'

She shrugged, 'Least my shot did some good.' She pointed towards the car she had hit, the alarm still singing into the late afternoon. A horde of undead were beginning to gather around it - distracted from their journey towards Rebecca and Chris' home.

'Whatever,' Chris set the crossbow down and - as his wife had done before him - replaced the window's flimsy barricade. 'You going to tell me where you got it?' he asked again.

'Does it really matter?'

'Why are you being so difficult?' Chris was used to her temper. Rebecca was four years older than him and had always been opinionated, angry, abrupt, bossy, dominant and - sometimes - even crude. Her hair was an auburn colour but her traits were definitely geared more towards a natural red-head. Even so - recently - she seemed to be getting worse.

She slumped down on the bed which had now become the sitting area - as well as still being the bed when the time came to sleep. 'I'm fed up with it all,' she hissed.

'What?'

'Everything. This whole existence!' She laughed, 'You know - back when I had to get up and go to work, I used to wish for stuff like this to happen. Well, you know what they say, be careful of what you wish for. Am I right?'

Before the world had gone to shit, Rebecca had worked for the company EE. Days spent sitting at a computer in the business department. During the quiet moments - and sometimes even in the busy ones - she had often day-dreamed of an end of the world situation. It wasn't the survival that she dreamed about, nor was it mental images of killing hordes of the infected. No, it was the whole "not having to get up for work" that she dreamed of. In hindsight, she could have just wished for another job or - better yet - a winning lottery ticket.

'Is this my fault?' she asked Chris.

'What? The outbreak?'

'Am I to blame? I wished for it and it came true. So it could well be my fault. Or it could all be a shitty dream from which I'll wake up any minute now. A new day and one where I'll be grateful for my life and that the end of the world hasn't happened.' She continued without taking a breath, 'Pinch me.'

'What?'

'I want to know if I am dreaming. Pinch me.'

'I'm not going to pinch you.'

'Just think - it's all a dream and the world hasn't ended.'

'Dave Grohl would still be alive,' Chris mused. He wasn't a homosexual but, if he were that way inclined, Grohl would be his man.

'That's all you can think about?'

'What can I say? I miss his music.'

'The world returns to normal and all you care about is Dave Grohl?'

Chris shrugged, 'What can I say? I'm a man of simple pleasures.' He turned the tables back to his wife before it got even more awkward, 'What about you? What do you miss?'

'My friends,' Rebecca answered without hesitation.

Rosie was the youngest of Rebecca's friends. Nearly ten years younger in fact but she was a good laugh. An innocent girl who enjoyed playing board games. Mel was a little older than Rebecca (a few months) and was the polar opposite of Rosie. She liked smoking rollies and drinking JD. A female Frank Gallagher; a total rule breaker who was just as crude as Rebecca and seemingly enjoyed going against the grain. Lisa was about ten years older, also a smoker, and good with her hands - in that she liked making things. And then, of course, there was Craig. Thirty-seven years old going on ten with his enjoyment and obvious love of practical jokes. Of the group, he could definitely be a dick but - even so - it didn't stop Rebecca missing him any less.

Rebecca looked at Chris and wondered whether it was her friends in particular that she missed or just... Someone different to talk to. Without knowing what she was thinking, he smiled at her sympathetically. Ignoring Grohl, there were things about "life" that he was missing too. The only difference was, he tried not to think about them as he knew it wouldn't do any good. If he was to survive then he knew he had to adapt to what living was all about now, not what it used to be. But then - who said he had to survive? Who said either of them had to survive? There was always the other option; one they had never spoken of despite it always being there for them.

Suicide.

'There are always other options,' he said carefully.

'What are you talking about?'

He shook his head, 'Nothing. Forget about it.'

'No. If you have something to say. You know I hate it when you do that.' She carried on clearly frustrated, 'You always do that - start to say something and then change your mind…' She pushed him again, 'What were you saying?'

He took the plunge, 'If you hate this whole existence, there's always the other option.'

'What are you talking about?'

'The *other* option.'

'Whatever is one your mind - will you just spit it out!'

'We could kill ourselves.'

Rebecca was stunned. She looked at him in disbelief but didn't know what to say. Once (once) she had thought about it but it had been a very fleeting thought. It wasn't in her nature to take her own life. It was one thing to hate an existence, quite another to pull the plug on it.

'Someone might yet come and help us,' she pointed out.

'Who?' He glanced over her shoulder towards the wall at the back of the room. Since all of this had begun, they had been etching little lines in the wall to help them keep track of how many days it had been. Looking at the wall, it was nigh on impossible to count the days at a glance now. Even so he tried to quickly tot it up on his head.

'Three hundred and eighty four days,' Rebecca said; no expression in her tone. She knew what Chris was doing. She could see him mentally counting thanks to the tell-tale sign of his eyes darting back and forth over the lines.

The exact date wasn't really necessary for his point anyway, 'No one is coming...' His mind flitted to the dead outside, the ones who'd soon be scraping on the door trying to get in for a feast of brain and flesh. He continued, 'At least - there's no one coming who can help us.'

'So what? You want to give up?' Rebecca couldn't tell if he was being serious or not. He could be witty from time to time but the way he was talking now - this was a first.

'You said it yourself - it's dangerous out there. If it's not the undead, it's the looters and other survivors. Before now you've even worried that it won't be the undead that kill us but other people instead. Living people like us, twisted and corrupted by what has become of the world.' He paused a moment, 'Really - is that the kind of world you want to live in because I - for one - would happily punch my ticket right now.'

'Stop talking like that, I don't like it.'

'So you're trying to tell me you don't feel the same?'

'No! I just get... Low from time to time.'

'Your friends are dead. My friends are dead. The world has gone to shit and it's only going to get worse as supplies get more scarce and those people who remain - breathing - get more desperate in how far they'll go to survive.' Chris shrugged, 'I don't want to see this.'

'So you want to kill yourself?'

'You think we'd be the only people to do it?'

'We'd come back as one of them. You want to be like that? I don't...'

'Shut up! Just shut up!'

'We could get some pills next time you're out and about. It would be just like going to sleep.'

Rebecca walked to the bedroom door and froze. She snorted, 'You know what I really hate about this new world?'

'What?'

'You can't storm out like you used to be able to. You can't just grab your keys and leave the house, jump in your car and drive off for a few hours.' She turned back into the room, 'You're stuck to face your arguments until one of you backs down.'

'I don't want to back down,' Chris shrugged.

'And I'm not ready to die,' Rebecca replied. She slumped down with her back against the wall. They both fell into an uncomfortable silence broken only by the occasional groaning from beyond the flimsy barricade over the window and the now irritating car alarm.

Chris was the first to break, 'Stuck together and the silent treatment too?' Rebecca looked at him; a cold glare. She didn't say anything though. 'Really?' Again, nothing but an icy stare. 'Well just so I know - how long is this going to go on for?'

'Until you stop talking like an idiot.'

The silence crept back into the room; an unwelcome visitor there to test the strength of the once-united couple. They'd been through so much since what was called *The End of Days* - this was the first time they'd encountered this scenario though. Sitting there now, in the uncomfortable silence, both of them were very aware that it had only ever been a matter of time until the topic of suicide raised its head. With limited options as to what to do with a life once a society had collapsed - it was one choice which had always been present, lurking in the background.

Rebecca didn't admit it but - before this very conversation - she had thought about it herself. It wasn't a long drawn out thought. Nothing was planned. It was just there, niggling at the back of her mind. It wasn't *death* it was *freedom* - and your own hand was definitely a better prospect than being ripped apart by a horde of flesh-eaters. The thought was back there again, closer to the forefront now though having been awakened by her husband. Maybe it was the right thing to do? Maybe it would be easier?

'Funny,' she said, 'I never thought today would end like this.'

Chris smiled, 'I kind of did.'

Silence.

'How would you kill yourself?' Rebecca asked.

'Pills? They say it is like going to sleep.'

'Really? Because whenever I see pictures of pill-suicides, the person always has their eyes open and is lying in their own vomit. I don't think it will be an easy death.'

'I couldn't cut myself,' Chris said all matter of fact. 'Maybe walk out to the river. Tie something heavy around my ankle and stroll in until I was totally submerged.' He continued, 'Drowning… People say that is like going to sleep.'

Rebecca laughed, 'How do these people know what it is like?'

Silence.

Chris shrugged.

'I wouldn't want to drown,' Rebecca continued. 'I wouldn't want to burn either. Or fall from a height.' A slight pause. She got up and walked back over to the seating area (bed) and sat down on the edge. The bed creaked. 'I hate heights,' she said.

The car alarm outside died.

Rebecca and Chris looked towards the window. Neither one of them said anything. Neither one of them were surprised by the sudden quietness out there.

That was the problem with this world; a problem which had been present in the last world too, before the shit hit the metaphorical fan - everything dies.

'I don't think I've ever said it but - I'm scared,' Rebecca said. 'I'm always scared, even when it's just the two of us in here. I'm always expecting something to happen, something to ruin things further. I don't mean to be pessimistic but…' She sighed, 'How else are you supposed to be in a world like this?'

Chris didn't say anything. He leaned close to her and gave her a soft, tender kiss on her cheek. He pulled back and looked her straight in the eye with a smile on his face, 'I love you,' he said.

'I love you too,' she smiled as her eyes welled up; not through sentiment but through fear. She'd clocked the knife in her husband's hand. She knew what was coming. Her moving across the room, to be closer to him, was her way of silently accepting it. The next world would be better. And besides, if she didn't accept it, the last thing she wanted was for him to go all *Jack Torrence* on her from *The Shining* and end up butchering her anyway, stabbing her in the back when she wasn't expecting it. He'd been getting stranger each day since he hurt his leg, to such an extent that she found herself wondering whether he'd banged his head at the same time.

'If we had music playing,' Chris said, 'I'd put *No Way Back* on now, by *The Foo Fighters.*'

Rebecca grinned, 'Why does that not surprise me?'

And - with that - he thrust forward with the knife, sticking it in her heart. She let out a gasp, her eyes went wide, her hands clenched into fists. Death's ice-cold embrace didn't take long to cradle her in His sweet arms. It was a quick death for the woman he loved but he knew it wasn't the end. As soon as the body was cold, he knew she'd open her eyes and her shell would come back with a taste for brains and flesh.

Of course, he could have left it there. He could have taken his own life with the same knife and just be done with it once and for all but… As previously mentioned, he couldn't cut himself. He'd have been a useless manic-depressive. Putting that to one side, though, he couldn't leave it there. He couldn't let her come back as one of them. She deserved better.

With teary eyes he pulled the knife from her chest and placed the tip of the blade against the middle of her skull. All he had to do was push down, through the skull and into her brain. A quick movement - with enough pressure - and that would be it. She wouldn't come back and he could set about figuring out how to join her with the least amount of pain.

Chris' grip tightened around the handle, he closed his eyes and took a deep breath. His whole body started to shake as he fought with the mind stopping him from seeing the action through.

'Shit.'

He pulled the knife away and repositioned it so that the blade's edge pressed up against her neck. If the head comes off - that stops them coming back, right? He was sure it would. The amount of films he'd seen where decapitation had worked in the films and wondered about it, he just never thought he'd be testing the method with his wife.

With the blade pushed down hard, he pulled the knife across her soft skin. The serrated teeth ate the skin open with relative ease and the blood started to spill. No spray, no over the top fountain of claret sprinkling the room in red - no chance of that happening with the lack of heartbeat.

Chris screamed, hating what he was having to do. He closed his eyes and started hacking backwards and forwards as quickly as he could, hoping to be able to cut through quickly just to get it over and done with. Two reasons for his speedy working; the first being he wanted it done so he could move on and the second - he didn't want her waking mid-cut and taking a bite out of his arm.

With the knife - backwards and forwards, backwards and forwards, backwards and forwards… He could feel Rebecca's head rocking with each pull back and push forward of the blade. He couldn't see the damage happening but he could hear it; ripping, squelching, squirting, tearing and - then - grinding and scraping as the metal hit and dragged across bone.

Chris gagged, scrunched his eyes tighter and worked at the bone harder and with more pressure applied.

'Come on, come on, come on,' he shouted with each motion of his arm. 'COME ON!' There was a final rip of flesh and the head rolled to the side as the knife finished passing through the body and hit upon the carpeted floor. Chris slowly opened his eyes and looked down. The head was away from the body as he'd expected. The eyes were staring straight at him; a lifeless, cold stare.

Chris gagged again and followed through, spewing up onto the carpet with a heavy heave. He coughed and wiped the back of his hand across his mouth, sweeping away the bitter-tasting spillage.

That's it now, he thought. *The worst is over with.*

But it wasn't though and he knew it wasn't as his eyes fixed upon the blade used to dispatch his wife. She was free but he wasn't. Not yet. He still needed to take his own life.

In an instant, he grabbed the knife and put it to his own neck - pressing the dirty blade hard against his own skin. He paused a moment. His hand, trembling. He just wanted it over with, his own death, but... Easier said than done.

He screamed again and pressed harder, yet still not hard enough to break the skin. Just as quickly as he'd put the knife against his throat, he pulled it away too. He didn't want to cut himself, he'd already made that clear to Rebecca but - even if he were able to do it... He didn't want to come back as one of *them*. He didn't want to walk the earth looking for flesh to feast upon.

Brain trauma stops that.

He put the tip of the blade up close to his eye. A sudden ramming motion would push the metal back through his head and into his brain. Hey presto! Brain trauma! He sat there a moment, staring at the tip of the blade. His hand still shaking, his heart racing.

Chris screamed again and threw the knife across the room. It hit the wall at the far side and dropped to the floor.

It's okay, he thought, *someone will come. Someone will find me. I don't need to do this... I don't...* He looked across to the body of Rebecca. His eyes welled-up. If he was too scared to follow her, if he was too scared to take his own life - he hadn't needed to take hers.

Outside the undead roamed freely in the street. Occasionally they'd groan or make a strange, gargled noise from the back of the throat as they lurched around with arms hanging by their sides and feet dragging on the ground. A scream of frustration and sadness - coming from the house at the far end of the street - penetrated the deathly air and the hordes of the undead stopped in their tracks momentarily. Slowly - one by one - they all looked in the direction of the scream. Slowly - one by one - they started their slow but definite movement towards the house and the source of the scream.

TO BE CONTINUED

CHAPTER FIVE

A WAY OUT

TODAY

Nicola burst into the third floor bedroom, startling James in the process, 'Scared the crap out of me,' he laughed.

'There's a cure,' she said - unable to contain her excitement.

'What?'

'There's a fucking cure!' she repeated. She stopped a moment when she noticed the carnage sprayed and squashed around the room, 'What the hell happened?'

James ignored her question and concentrated on her initial statement, 'A cure? What are you talking about - a fucking cure? How? Who?'

'There's someone downstairs - in the lock-up... They were brought in late yesterday...' Nicola stepped into the room and closed the bedroom door behind her. 'One of them has a bite.'

'And they haven't turned? How is that possible?'

'Because - as far as I can tell - it's a living human bite. It's not a bite from one of the undead.' Nicola and James had seen enough bites in their time to know that the look is very different to the look of a bite from a living person. For one, when you're bitten by the living - there is less puss. Much, much less puss. And the skin doesn't turn black and angry around the wound. But - Frank had no medical knowledge whatsoever and didn't know that it wouldn't be possible for this to be a "cured" zombie bite and that's the way Nicola wanted to keep it.

'I don't get it. You said there was a cure,' James said.

'And that's what Frank thinks too,' Nicola spoke in a quieter tone.

'I'm sorry - I really don't get it.'

'I know you're not happy here. I've seen the way you squirm when they bring someone new into their sick games. I feel the same. And if Frank thinks this person is a cure to everything - he'll let them go but, because he'll want to take the praise for getting them to wherever they need to get safely, he'll send a small team up North with them. We're the medics. We can be on that team but - first - you need to confirm what I say... That it looks as though the man is the cure.'

James was unhappy in the house but - unlike Nicola - he thought he was the only one who felt like this. Everyone else seemed content with what was going on. God knows enough people showed up to the Fight Clubs to show their support for what was happening; a brutal death match that took place, between kidnapped survivors, down in the basement on a weekly basis; the one that Gina was currently champion of. Then - of course - there was the number of people who frequented the girls on the third floor... It was no surprise James felt alone in his wish to escape the house and yet - in such a short space of time - he was one of three who wanted out and who was prepared to put everything on the line to get out.

* * * * *

Christina walked into Gina's room with the tray of meat plated-up as per her usual daily task. Judging by the way she walked with a slight limp, she'd already made good on her other task; serving Frank, or rather - letting Frank ejaculate in her arsehole.

Christina didn't say anything to Gina. She set the plate down next to where Gina rested back against the wall and - with a wink - left the room, closing the door behind her. Gina picked the slab of meat up and went to take a bite, only stopping when she realised that there - beneath it - was a small key. The key to the restraints keeping her tethered to the wall.

Was this a test?

Gina glanced up at the door half-expecting it to suddenly open and Frank to enter - laughing at his cruel joke, teasing Gina with the possibility of freedom. Only when she realised the door wasn't opening did she grab the key. Immediately she slotted it into the padlock's keyhole. She went to twist the key, popping the lock open, but suddenly froze. What if this was nothing to do with Christina trying to free both Gina and herself from this Hell House? What if this was all part of a plan put in motion by Frank? What if Christina had been told to give her the key? Gina knew that if she freed herself with the key and went to escape it would give Frank the perfect excuse to kill her without going back on the supposed promise he had made. The promise of freedom after winning ten fights in his sick and twisted games.

Gina was frozen on the spot. Her mind torn in two. On the one hand she wanted to turn the key, pop the lock and run - without looking back. Consequences be damned. On the other hand… One more fight and he'd have to prove to the rest of the house that he was lying all along and that he never had any intention of releasing anyone after ten wins. But then - if he turned around and killed her after her tenth win - would anyone in the house give a fuck? And that's supposing she even won the next fight.

Of course she'd win.

Forgetting the first fight - that was a completely different bag of bones - the other fights were all easier. Once you've beaten the first person to death, the rest seem like nothing in comparison and - even if they hadn't been - Gina always had the upper hand in the other fights anyway. After all, the people she was fighting were new to the experience, they still thought they could talk their way out of the mess and - when trying to do just that - she landed the first blow to the throat; a move she learned from the first fight. A quick jab to the throat causes the other person to choke and - during that time - you go for the eyes. Take their breath away, take their sight away - after that, as they continue choking, it's an easy win.

As Gina contemplated staying - and letting it play out as fate intended - her mind played a quick recap through the lives she had already taken. The first life being that of her old friend, Ellie -

a pretty girl with blonde hair and blue eyes who was reduced to a bloody mess at the hands of Gina who screamed with every blow she landed upon her friend. By the time she was done, the pretty blue eyes were missing, the blonde hair was tainted red and the face was unrecognisable as human.

The crowd loved it.

The crowd loved it.

Forty people, or thereabouts, all screaming and cheering - waving betting slips around in the air as Gina murdered her friend. Thinking back to their reaction, there is no way they would give a shit if Frank suddenly turned on Gina if she were the victor for the tenth time. They liked the blood. They got off on the carnage.

Snapping back to reality Gina knew - if she didn't seize this opportunity - she was dead.

She turned the key in the lock.

* * * * *

Frank watched from the doorway as James and Nicola inspected the bite on Mathew's stomach once more. James turned to Frank and nodded, 'I agree with Nicola. He should have turned. How he didn't... Well...' He shrugged. 'He's immune. Somehow his blood holds a cure for it.' James stood up and walked over to Frank, followed by Nicola, 'If they're on their way North - we need to make sure they get there.'

Frank nodded slowly and then smiled, 'I'm not saying I don't believe you,' Frank said with careful thought, 'but - saving getting our hopes up and wasting all that fuel and resources to get him up to the government facility... How's about we test him? You know - just to be sure.'

'That's not a good idea,' Nicola spoke up quickly.

'Is it not?' Frank asked. He wasn't surprised that there might have been a problem.

'They'll want his blood to be as pure as possible,' she thought on her feet. 'If we expose him to another bite…'

Frank nodded, 'I understand.' He paused and then smiled again. 'So we'll get them up to where they need to go then. Probably best that we send a couple of people with them, yeah? Make sure they get there safely…'

James started to get uncomfortable with Frank's tone. This was all too easy. 'Only if you think it's necessary,' James said. 'I mean - can we spare anyone from the house?'

Nicola was blinded by her desperation to get out of the house and hadn't sensed the dangerous mood of Frank, 'We'll have to go,' she said. 'Me and James. I mean - if something happens on the way - he needs someone who'll be able to help him.'

'I see.' Frank grinned. 'I guess we can all go.'

'There's no point you going,' Nicola said. 'You need to stay here and keep control of the house. People rely on you…'

'Yes, that's true but…' Frank pointed to Mathew who - sensibly enough - was staying quiet, as was Stacey. 'The world is relying on us to deliver him to…' he stopped talking - worrying both James and Nicola. They knew he didn't just stop talking unless something was really bugging him.

'What is it?' Nicola asked, trying to stay calm.

'Him. He is the cure.' Frank turned to Stacey, 'You're not a cure. You're just another mouth to feed. We don't need you. The world doesn't need you.' Frank reached behind him and pulled his knife back out from between belt and jeans. Stacey screamed and huddled into the corner of the room - as far away as the chains permitted.

'Wait!' James called out. 'Why waste her? You still have the other woman in the next room. You can carry on with your plans to have the fight. No sense just wasting her life like this…'

'Really?' Frank sighs. 'I don't know why but… I just feel like… Yeah… Something is bugging me. I think… I just don't like being lied to you know…'

'Who is lying to you?'

Frank turned his attention away from a clearly nervous Stacey and stared - unblinking - at James, 'All of you,' he said quietly.

CHAPTER SIX

SECRETS AND LIES

6 MONTHS AGO

The old oak door opened and Frank stepped into what must have been the master bedroom. Large television against the far wall, huge four poster-bed sitting in the centre of the room, cupboards - solid oak - up against another of the four walls and - opposite these - a bookcase seemingly filled with novels of all shapes and sizes. Despite the chaos outside, the room was immaculate and clearly looked after.

Frank walked over to the bookcase and wasn't surprised to find a number of titles he deemed to be pretentious; authors such as Charles Dickens, William Shakespeare, George Orwell and - tucked in the corner looking very much out of place - Stuart Keane with a clean, new looking book which was a stark contrast to the dusty looking first editions that went before it.

'What the fuck…' Frank reached out and tried to pull the Keane book from the case. To his surprise it didn't budge other than to tilt slightly; a tilting which was accompanied by a loud whirring noise. Confused, he stepped back and watched in awe as the bookcase opened up to reveal a secret room. 'What the actual fuck,' Frank said quietly before laughing to himself, 'Fucking rich people.'

The door stopped moving and revealed the room on the other side; a safe room for times of trouble - installed into the homes of the paranoid and rich. The far wall was lined with security monitors - all powered by the same generator that fed the rest of the mansion - capturing each and every room and all that happened within, recording directly to a hard drive.

'Interesting…'

Frank took a seat in the black leather office chair which was parked in front of the monitors. Making himself comfortable, he started looking from screen to screen. A smile on his face thanks to the smug feeling of being in complete control; he could see his housemates and they couldn't see him.

Glancing down at the control panels attached to the desk before him, he started fiddling with the various knobs; one of which controlled the sound for the room currently displayed on the main screen - one of the smaller bedrooms.

'This place is fucking insane,' said one of the men. A greasy looking thirty year old with long, dark hair and a heavily knotted beard. 'Far fucking cry from the council estate I grew up on.'

'I wonder what his plan is now we're in here,' the second of the men said.

'No idea and - I'll be honest - I don't really give a fuck at the moment… I just want one night to sleep in a comfortable bed, you know?'

'I hear that.'

Frank pressed a button flicking both the sound and the main screen to another room.

'What the fuck?' he muttered to himself.

On screen there was a group of about four men of various sizes. They were in another bedroom - a larger room with a similar four-post bed to the room Frank had been investigating. The bed was not unoccupied though. Strapped by his wrists, there appeared to be a man trussed up there with a black leather hood covering his face, his body naked other than a pair of black latex shorts. The man was alive, seemingly looking between the gawping men despite not being able to see through the hood. One of the men had a wallet in his hands, found amongst the pile of clothes littered on the floor next to the bed.

'Iain Rob Wright,' the man said - looking at the driving licence.

'Is that cum on his belly?' a second man asked - noticing the suspicious looking gloop on Iain's stomach, pooling in his belly button as well as being splashed further up his stomach and chest. 'That's cum. That is fucking disgusting.'

'Looks fresh. Maybe he and the owner were having a little party in here before we interrupted?' Addressing Iain, 'That what happened, faggot? So - what - you the sub and he was the Master?'

'Seem to know a lot about this,' a third man joked.

Man two, 'Fuck you.'

Man one, 'He isn't saying much.'

Man two, 'Maybe he needs his Master's permission to speak?'

Man four - joining in, 'Long fucking wait to hear him talk again.'

Four men laugh.

Man two, 'Might have a gag in his mouth.'

Man three, 'You really do know a lot about this...'

Man two, 'Seriously. Fuck you.'

Man four, 'Take the hood off.'

Man two, 'Me? You take the fucking hood off.'

Man three, 'Get out of the way.'

On screen - the third man of the group pushed past the others and approached the bed. The hooded pervert heard him approach and looked in his direction. With a visibly shaking hand, the man reached out and took a hold of the hood. Seemingly counting down from three to one, without saying the words, he suddenly pulled the hood up and away from the trussed up slave. All four men jumped back in shock when they realized that the pervert was one of the undead. With the hood off, and able to see the four meal tickets - the slave started pulling at the restraints, snarling and biting towards the men despite not being able to move. Only when they realised they were safe did the four men start to laugh - as did Frank who'd been glued to the screen the whole time.

Man one, 'Question is - has this happened since The Master made him look like a plasterer's radio or was the Master taking advantage of someone unable to say no?'

Man three, 'That's fucking sick.'

Man four, 'I don't know… Catch them when they're still warm and - so long as you cover the mouth - it could be like fucking one of the living.'

Man three, 'You're not right in the head.'

Man four, 'You telling me that - if there was this big-titted bitch trussed up in front of you like this… You wouldn't fuck her?'

Man three, 'She dead?'

Man four, 'Undead.'

Man three, 'Then no… No I wouldn't. I mean… What if this thing is transmittable the same way AIDS is?'

Man four, 'Protection to be safe. Bareback if you want to risk it.'

Man three, 'Seriously - I got to fucking share a house with you?'

Man two, 'I'd do it. Yeah. I'd fuck her.'

Man three, 'Well I wouldn't.'

Man four, 'I see what the problem is…'

Man three, 'What?'

Man four casually strolled over to the rotting dead fuck and, with both hands, yanked the latex shorts down exposing the man's cock. He grabbed it with one hand and turned back to the disgusted third man in the group, 'This is more your thing, isn't it?' he asked - pointing the flaccid penis in the direction of the man he was addressing. 'Come on… Come and give it a suck… You know you want to.' He started tugging on it, 'Might even be able to get it hard if you want a ride…'

Man one and Man two were laughing. Man three shook his head, 'You need fucking help.' And - with that - he stormed from the room. Man one and Man two - still laughing - followed.

Man two (on his way out the door and talking to man four), 'You might want to sort him out.'

By 'sort him out' he meant for his colleague to put the slave out of its misery - a heavy blow to the frontal lobe, or with something going through the brain. He knew what he meant and so did the man he was addressing and yet - somehow - it was lost in translation. Man four, still laughing, called out, 'You can't knock it until you've tried it!' He then - licking his lips - leaned down and wrapped his mouth around the still flaccid penis.

'Fuck sake!' Frank switched to another room to save witnessing anything else.

Two people were sitting in what looked to be an office. One of them was behind a desk, rooting through the drawers whilst another - Colleen Cassidy - was sitting opposite staring at the other person.

'What do you think he will do for us?' Colleen asked. 'I mean - now we are in here... Do you think he has a plan or do you think he is just going to wing it and - another point - how do we know we can trust him?' It was a similar conversation to the one Frank had eaves-dropped in on previously; his plan and leadership skills being called into question. Something which - actually - insulted Frank a little. He had promised them a safe haven, he had delivered a safe haven. Yet they still had the audacity to question him.

'I guess,' the second person said, 'we'll have to wait and see.'

'What if we don't have to wait and see? We could take the house for ourselves.'

Frank sat up, leaning closer to the television screen - his curiosity piqued.

'We don't owe him anything,' the woman continued. 'We could take the house for ourselves... If we're clever about it... We can get rid of the others too before they even know what is happening.'

'And how do you suppose we do that?' the man stopped rooting through the drawers and pushed them shut.

'There's a kitchen… I could take a knife… Seduce him… You've seen the way he has been looking at me… Then - when we're alone…'

'You're going to stab him?'

Colleen shrugged, 'It would work. He wouldn't see it coming.'

Frank smiled, 'Oh really?'

CHAPTER SEVEN

KNOWING WHEN TO QUIT

TODAY

It had been six months since Frank had stuck the knife into Colleen's cold heart. The two of them had been alone in the room he'd chosen to be his bedroom; the same room that led onto the safe room. She had taken her top off, revealing her pert breasts. She had been smiling at him, unaware that he had exactly the same plan she had in her own mind. See, she was expecting him to come forward to fondle her and - when he did - that was when she would have struck. As it was, he waited for her to come closer to him and *that* was when he had struck her. He had pulled the knife out of her chest and she had bled out within minutes. Her own weapon was found tucked down the back of her shiny leggings; another one of the kitchen knives.

Six months. How time flies and here he was again - a knife in hand with the pointy end sticking in one of his supposedly-trusted housemates.

James was gasping for air. Shock on his face. He hadn't seen the attack coming until it was too late. He should have expected it. He had seen Frank's temper before and had known he was unpredictable. Nicola and Stacey were both screaming whereas Mathew was surprisingly quiet. Frank pulled the knife out and turned his back on James who dropped to his knees, clutching the fresh wound.

Frank lifted a bloody finger to his lips and shushed the girls quiet.

'No sense crying over spilt blood,' he smiled.

Nicola rushed over to James' side and put her hands down on the hole in his chest - trying to stem the bleeding.

'He's dead already,' Frank said. 'Well, okay, he's not dead yet but he'll be dead soon enough and we both know the cunt deserved it. You all fucking deserved it.' He pointed to Stacey, 'You're a lying piece of shit, you deserve to die.' He pointed to Mathew, 'You're just a waste of fucking oxygen…'

'Fuck you.'

And then Frank pointed to Nicola, 'And you - disloyal cunt just like James is.'

James let out a final breath.

Frank corrected himself, 'Was. A disloyal cunt just like James *was*.'

'You fucking killed him!' Nicola screamed.

Frank looked down at the man he'd shared many a drink with - a mixture of bitter disappointment and contentment; the latter being something he felt every time he murdered one of those who were against him. The disappointment came not from the fact he'd shared drinks with him, but more so because James died never knowing how Frank knew so much.

The group thought Frank drunk himself unconscious every night but it wasn't the case. That was just the act he put on so he could be left alone. An act he had put on since first discovering the secret room.

Every evening was the same, he'd take Christina to his bedroom along with a bottle of Scotch. He'd fuck her - any which way he chose, open the bottle and then kick her out of the room - back to her own sleeping quarters that she shared with the other (vastly out-numbered) females. Then - and only then - he'd close the door and retire into his safe room for the rest of the night; watching the housemates as they fucked the dead, discussed the many fight clubs, chatting shit or - finally - conspired against him.

Frank shrugged, *Well what's done is done.*

He turned to Nicola, 'You've been a very, very naughty little girl.'

'I don't know what you're talking about.'

Frank walked over to the door, ensuring the way was blocked for Nicola. He turned back to Nicola and warned her, 'The bite on that fat fuck,' he said - pointing to Mathew, 'might be fake but in the next ten minutes or so, *that* fuck,' he pointed to James, 'is going to open his eyes and sit up. And - when he does - he's going to be fucking hungry.' Frank paused a moment, 'I have to confess to being curious as to which one of you three he will eat first.' He suddenly shrugged, 'Fuck knows. Anyway, if you'll excuse me... I'm needed elsewhere.' He gave a final smile to the people in the room and then stepped out into the hallway - closing the door behind him and dead-bolting it.

Nicola ran over to the door and started hitting it, hoping to break through. No joy.

'You can't leave us in here!' she screamed again and again.

Mathew and Stacey, meanwhile, looked towards James and waited - nervously. They both knew, if he weren't dealt with soon - Frank was right - he would turn and he would have a feast on his hands.

Meanwhile - on the other side of the door - Frank found himself struggling with regards to what to do next. He knew Christina had betrayed him, partly why he had insisted upon the arsehole that morning, and he knew Gina had the key to her freedom hidden beneath her meal. He also knew he could charge into the room and get the key back before she had a chance to use it and - then - he could snap Christina's neck before letting her turn; another dead whore for the fuck floor. She was fun to fuck whilst breathing, he was sure the lads would have just as much fun with her when she wasn't breathing too. The only reason he didn't follow through with either action was because he was growing tired of the people setting out to topple him from his position as the head of the house, or even those who were just ungrateful as to the roof he had provided for them.

Part of him thought it might be better if Gina did escape and if he let her kill as many of the housemates as she could, on her way to freedom. Cleanse the house and start again with people who respected him and all he did for them. Or - better yet - let every fucker die and he could live there alone, in peace and quiet without having to spend every near-sleepless night staring at a series of computer monitors.

It was just *knowing when to quit.*

Frank looked down the hallway to where Gina's room was. The door was still shut so she hadn't escaped yet.

Just a matter of time, he thought to himself.

After a brief moment of hesitation, he turned and walked away - heading back to his own room. Fuck them. Fuck them all to Hell. He created this little society, therefore he got to choose when it came to an end and now seemed like a good time.

As he turned the corner he literally bumped into Christina.

'Sorry - I didn't see you there,' she said sheepishly. She had been loitering close to Gina's room - ready to run with her as soon as she came out of the room.

'What are you doing hanging about here?' Frank asked even though he knew the answer. He was more interested in hearing her excuse as to why she had a black rucksack slung over her shoulder; something she tried to subtly hide by backing up against the wall.

'I've just fed the lady in the end hallway,' Christina lied. Frank knew it was a lie. After Nicola went off to fetch James, in order to get him to check the bite, Frank had run back to his safe room to watch what everyone said via the hidden cameras. Out of the corner of his eye, on one of the smaller screens, he witnessed Christina take the woman her food as he overheard the other liars - James and Nicola - discussing their way out of the house.

'Running late today,' Frank smiled. He was undecided as to what to do with Christina. She was a treacherous bitch for sure but... Damn she had a sweet tasting pussy. Be a shame to taint that with the possibly unhealthy taste of rot when there was a chance he could convince her that sticking with him was the best option.

She smiled sweetly at him, 'I'm sorry. I dozed off after earlier,' she said - referring to the sexual encounter she had had with Frank earlier in the morning. 'I was so tired.'

He laughed, 'I don't blame you.' A pause as he contemplated asking about the bag, 'Still - it's not as though she was going to starve by waiting a little while longer for her dinner. No harm, no foul.' Realising time was against him now - what with the woman's imminent escape and James' potential turn, 'If you excuse me… Something to take care of.' He side-stepped her and continued on his way back to the safe room - all the time thinking about how easy people found lying to him. A house full of traitors, liars and ungrateful cunts.

This wasn't how it was supposed to be.

Fuck them all. Fuck them all to Hell. Even Christina.

She unleashed the storm that was coming, she will get what she deserves, he thought as he started down the stairs towards his room. *Fuck her. Fuck her - metaphorically - and then fuck her literally.*

CHAPTER EIGHT

BEST LAID PLANS

6 MONTHS AGO

Frank was standing in front of the other housemates; a group of twenty mixed between men and women - the ratio more in favour of males. Frank would have preferred it to be the other way round; more women than men. Truth be told, most of the other (male) housemates would have probably preferred that to be the case too but it was never spoken out loud and neither was it discussed as to why it happened to fall like this. Thinking to himself, Frank presumed men just made better survivors than women - hence the majority of the women they stumbled across, out there in the real world, were already dead. Whatever the reason - and whoever was living here now - there was no sense dwelling on it. This was the way it was and this was who they had to live with now.

'You should have all been assigned a room by now,' Frank spoke out to the group, standing on the second floor and calling down to where they gathered in the main atrium - on the ground level. The rooms had been divided up fairly with most people sharing four to a room - sometimes more if the room was bigger. Obviously there weren't enough beds to go around so it was decided people would be sharing beds while others slept on the floor, or other furniture, and then - after a few days - they would swap, so all had a chance of comfort.

A muttered voice from below him distracted Frank enough to make him pause and look to the person responsible; a scrawny little fuck who - if Frank was being honest - he thought wouldn't have made it this far.

'Did you have something to say?' Frank asked.

'I just said, I don't understand why we aren't staying in the bedrooms up there,' a lone voice called up to the second floor. 'I mean, there are bedrooms up there. Down here - we're sleeping in office spaces, or a dining room or living room… It just feels pointless moving things around when we could just sleep up there…' The loner went quiet, aware that he was waffling.

'You could also sleep outside,' Frank reminded him. 'If you're not happy with this house, or how I choose to run it - by all means - fuck off.'

Keeping the people on the ground floor made sense to Frank. It kept them all close together in case of an emergency. Say, for instance, someone tried to break in (whether they be living or dead) - everyone would be on hand to help fend off the threat or even *hear* it at the very least and then be able to raise an alarm. If everyone was staying upstairs - there was no guarantee that they'd hear someone trying to break in or that they'd get down in time to help the others fend the intruder off before something bad happened. Frank could have explained this - and probably should have - but he figured it was common sense.

Frank continued, 'I have big plans for this little group of ours and I know some of you have been questioning one another as to what my plans may be. Well…' He smiled, 'We're going to have a fun loving atmosphere. We're going to have games, we're going to have fucking orgies - we're going to party without a care in the fucking world, just as we used to before things turned to shit. Basically - we're going to have the times of our lives whilst we wait for the help to arrive.' Frank grinned from ear to ear - excited at the prospect of finally turning his life back to fun and games, just as it used to be.

No one said anything. They were simply standing there with stunned expressions on their faces, with the exception of Colleen who was staring straight at Frank; a wicked twinkle in her eyes that Frank understood perfectly thanks to seeing her on the monitor. She gave him a wink and licked her lips seductively. Frank put her to the back of her mind. She was a threat but not an imminent one. First - deal with the rest of the house. Make them feel comfortable; something that wasn't going quite as he had imagined as Frank realised they didn't look half as enthused as he was. More than that - he realised some of them even looked concerned. His grin slowly disappeared from his face.

'That isn't good enough for you?' he asked. 'You want more?'

A voice called up. It was James. 'We're going to need food... Supplies...'

Frank shrugged, 'Then we will organise supply runs. On the other side of the woods - a four mile walk or so... You know where the shops are.'

'And do we make room for people we might find?' James called up. Frank looked at him blankly. James continued, 'Fellow survivors. Do we bring them back here? Make them part of this?'

* * * * *

The restraints dropped to the floor with a clatter as Gina finally used the key to free herself. She immediately looked up to the doorway half-expecting someone to come running in to see what the noise was. To her relief, no one did come in. She stood up, her joints cracking in the process thanks to so many uncomfortable hours chained to the wall with not much movement permitted.

Unaware of the hidden camera capturing her every movement, she crossed the room and pressed her ear to the door. There, she listened out for anything that might cause a problem should she open it. Nothing. Not a sound. A good omen? Or - they know she is readying her escape and they're out there, quietly waiting - tools at the ready.

Only one way to know for definite. Only one way to get out of this house and back to her family... Are they out there? She never saw them die. They could still be out there! They could be holed up somewhere, waiting for her. She reached out for the handle - only one way to find out and that involves opening the door.

She turned the handle and slowly pulled the door open and peered out. Gone was the ferocious fighting machine they'd created and back was the nervous woman they first met when they pulled her from her world and dragged her into this shit-hole.

To her relief, no one was standing there.

A glance down the hallway and she noticed Christina was standing there, motioning for Gina to go towards her.

'This way,' Christina whispered.

Overly cautious, she glanced over her shoulder. No one standing there, ready to hit her. She looked back to Christina who was still motioning for her to go towards her.

'This way,' Christina said again - still hushed.

Satisfied she was in no immediate danger, Gina rushed towards Christina. Instead of following her to safety though she grabbed her by the side of her head and slammed it against the wall. Unbeknownst to both women, Frank cheered.

Bitch got what she deserved.

CHAPTER NINE

THE BEGINNING OF THE END

6 MONTHS AGO

Colleen opened her eyes and immediately fixed her gaze upon the man on top of her. She didn't recognise him but that was to be expected. She didn't recognise anyone and neither did she feel pain from the wound to her chest - administered by the kitchen knife Frank plunged into her.

'Oh shit!' the man jumped off her and pulled his trousers up.

He backed himself into the corner of the garage as what-used-to-be Colleen sat up, snarling and gnashing with her teeth. She rolled off the work bench and landed on the floor with a thud.

'Oh fuck. I'm sorry. I'm sorry,' the man said over and over again as the recently-deceased Colleen clambered back up to her feet. 'It's not what you think!' the man continued. Actually it was exactly what Colleen would have thought, had she had the ability to think. The idea of sleeping with the dead put there when he'd stumbled into the room with the trussed up slave and was presented with the question, *would you sleep with the dead given half the chance?*

'It wasn't my idea,' the man said. 'They put me up to it…'

Colleen didn't stop for a conversation as she started lurching her way towards the man, her left foot dragging on the floor at an awkward angle.

'Stay back there. Don't come any closer.'

The door behind Colleen opened and Frank barged in with a metal bar in hand. Without a word, he ran up behind the girl he'd already killed once and - in one fluid movement - slammed the bar into her side, dropping her to the floor with a satisfying crack from her ribs. She wasn't dead (again), just stunned long enough for the man to run out of the room. Shaking his head - Frank followed and closed the garage door, sealing Colleen in once more.

'Thank you! Thank you!' the man kept saying over and over again. His face was pale - as though he were close to slipping into shock. 'She was going to bite me… I went in there because I heard something…' he started to make excuses as to why he *had been* in there.

Frank silenced him with a raised finger, 'I'm not here to judge,' he said. 'We all have needs but,' he continued, 'if you want to fulfil those needs - and again, I'm not here to judge, there are ways of doing it without risking your fucking neck and the lives of those who live in this house. You understand me?'

'Thank you. I'm sorry. I never meant…'

Frank silenced him with a raised finger once more.

'What's your name?' Frank asked.

'Chad. We met a couple of days ago. Chad Ferguson.'

'Well - Chad - if you want to do a little supply run for me… Take a couple of your friends… We can make it so you can fuck these *things* without putting yourself at risk to infection.'

'I don't know what you're talking…'

Again, a raised finger silenced him.

Frank continued, 'Sound like a plan?'

Chad nodded, 'Yes.'

Frank smiled, 'I'll write you a list.'

* * * * *

TODAY

Frank watched from the comfort of his safe room as Christina got back up from where she'd landed on the hallway floor, blood streaming down her face. Gina was long gone from the shot, just as the breath from Christina's body was. Frank had protected people from the undead before now, such as that time in the garage with Colleen's recently deceased corpse. But those days were gone. This was the great purge and he had front row seats.

He just wished he had some popcorn so he could really enjoy what was to come.

'They fucking deserve it,' he told himself. 'Each and every one of them. They all fucking deserve it.'

Frank didn't want to be alone. That's how the lie first started; a little white lie stating he knew a place where everyone would be safe. And then - when he got them here - a promise of fun whilst they waited for the real help to arrive in the form of the government bodies. Fun? Maybe he should have tried offering them something else? Spying on the group though, he knew he had to offer them something appealing and non-threatening. So many supposed-private conversations from people he brought here - all wanting to overthrow him. He figured - offer them fun and they'd be less willing to kill him. Give them exactly what they wanted and maybe they'd fall in line behind him? They want to fuck the dead? He can make that happen. They want to bet on people fighting? He can make that happen.

Hell. He *did* make it happen. He became the bad guy to give them what they wanted and he felt sick because of it.

And look how that turned out? He became something *they* created and now people were wanting to break out and make it on their own because they didn't like the monster they created. But that couldn't happen; them breaking out. He couldn't let them come and go as they pleased. He couldn't have an open door policy to the mansion. It posed too many problems and too many dangers from the outside world, not that he cared about them. But to put his own life in danger? No. Not a chance.

They deserve this, he thought to himself as he followed the recently-murdered Christina around the house - flicking from screen to screen to keep her on the centre display. Watching her - as she approached the first unsuspecting housemates; both of whom had their backs to her.

They deserve this.

On screen he watched as Christina bit into the back of the first victim's neck. The second person screamed and ran, just as many others would have done too thanks to the fight or flight rush surging through them.

Frank laughed.

They deserve this.

The first man bitten went down like a sack of shit with Christina dropped down with him so that she could carry on feasting upon the twitching body. Frank didn't take his eyes from the centre screen - mesmerised by how Christina was literally ripping into the man's guts, pulling out handfuls and handfuls of stringy intestine even though it wasn't the only act of extreme violence happening within the house...

* * * * *

Mathew repeatedly brought the heel of his shoe down upon James' face; a heavy Dr. Martin boot pummelling the now-dead man. Neither Nicola nor Stacey were watching as the boot finally caved James' skull in before following through and mashing the brain too, the danger of James sitting up as one of the undead now gone thanks to the excessive brain damage caused by the boot heel.

'It's done,' Mathew said - out of breath.

The girls looked over to the mess he'd made. Brain, skull, blood and clumps of hair splattered around where he was still attached to the wall by the chains.

Still wheezing - Mathew continued, 'Now we just need to figure a way out of the room.' He looked at Nicola, 'I don't suppose you have a key for the door?'

'It's not locked like that,' she said sheepishly. She was embarrassed about being in the room with the two prisoners. A part of her was worried that they might have honestly believed she had anything to do with their predicament. She set the record straight, 'This is nothing to do with me,' she said. She wasn't lying. She was one of the good ones. 'Not all of us are into this kind of thing. Some of us found this place and thought it was a safe haven. It was only when we were accepted into the ranks - because of skills we possessed - that we realised the truth and, by then, it was too late. To try and leave was to condemn yourself to death.'

'But you're fine to watch others get condemned?' Mathew retorted. 'And skills? What skills have you got? Certainly not acting skills, that's for sure. You must have done something to make him realise you were lying…'

Nicola didn't argue with the man. There was no point. She felt bad for them being here in the first place. She didn't see them as the enemy and didn't want to make them as such either.

Mathew realised she had gone quiet on him and pushed in another direction, 'So how is the door locked then? Do you think you can open by throwing your weight against it?'

Weight? The girl was about eleven stone at a push, certainly not much of her to use as a battering ram. That was one good thing about the apocalypse; obesity was at an all-time low. Harder to get fat when you're constantly running and food supplies are starting to dwindle.

'It's dead-bolted,' she said quietly.

'Bang on it,' Stacey said. 'Just because he wants you dead, there's so many other people in the house - someone might be around that doesn't know of his earlier intentions.'

Nicola doubted it somehow but given the fact there were no windows in the room and there was no other way to get out - there really was nothing to lose. Worst case, it might just bring Frank back in but at least if that happened - they could have it out finally as opposed to being left to starve to death.

'What kind of fucking circus you animals running here anyway?' Mathew huffed, still very much blaming Nicola for what was happening. Instead of answering him, she started hitting the door and calling out for help in the hope that someone would come and open the door for them.

Someone.

Anyone.

Maybe not Frank.

CHAPTER TEN

BLOODBATH

'Here we go again… This is it… Any minute now…' Frank leaned closer to the monitor to get a better view of the incoming carnage. Christina was approaching the back of another of the unsuspecting housemates; some waste of space who'd done very little to help around the house. The young man was leaning there, against a wall, listening to his headset.

Frank winced as Christina sunk her teeth into the man's neck causing a spray of red to paint the magnolia walls of the hallway. Just as the previous victim went down like a sack of shit, so did this victim. And speaking of the previous victim; on the monitor screen to the left of the one showing Christina greedily feasting, her half-munched first victim was starting to twitch as some kind of life started pumping back through the veins.

Frank sang to himself, 'Dum, dum, dum, another one bites the dust…' He suddenly stopped singing as he remembered the fact he had left Nicola in a room with a dead man. Surely he should be due to move soon enough? A few button presses and the screen changed to the room where he'd left Nicola. 'What the fuck?' He noticed there was no possibility of James turning as his head had been smashed in, 'For fuck sake.'

Nicola was banging on the door, 'Someone open the door! Please! Someone! Anyone!'

'Fucking bitch,' Frank muttered - disappointed he wasn't tuning in to watch her get pulled limb from limb by a newly hungry James. What annoyed Frank even more that - given what was happening out in the hallway - that room was actually one of the safest places to be at the moment. The undead might have been able to sneak up on people, catching them off guard but - as of yet - they haven't managed to undo door locks.

He shrugged the frustration off. When the house is clear, it just meant he could go and let her out of the room and - then - kill her himself. He smiled as the thought evolved a little more with little encouragement; and then he would wait for her to open her eyes once more - as one of the undead - and he would get to kill her all over again. See, there are perks to this virus. He chuckled to himself, half-wishing he had someone there with him to share this idea with.

A *clunk* from the screen snatched his attention back to what was happening as someone slid the bolt across from the other side of the room.

'What? No, no, no…' In that split second he had already built the idea up in his head, of getting to kill her twice and - now - that was about to be snatched away from him. 'Don't let the bitch out,' he whined like a spoiled child.

* * * * *

'Thank you!' Nicola said as she stepped back from the door - already thanking the person on the other side of it for undoing the lock. The door opened faster than anyone in the room had expected it and - quick as a flash - Gina charged in, slamming her weight against Nicola. The two girls dropped to the floor in a crumpled heap; Gina on top of Nicola. 'Get off me!' Nicola screamed out loud - not that Gina heard her, or - at the very least - paid her any kind of attention.

Still with her weight pinning Nicola down on the floor, Gina grabbed the stunned woman's head, her thumbs lined up perfectly to her eyeballs. Both Mathew and Stacey were trying to move themselves away from the mayhem by backing as close to their corner of the room as the chains would permit. Gina was screaming. Nicola was screaming - a scream that would change in pitch a second later as Gina pushed her thumbs down, behind Nicola's eyeballs and into her brain. And then - seconds later - the screaming stopped.

Gina pulled her fingers from out of the dead girl's skull and immediately looked up to Stacey first and then across the room to Mathew. Neither one of them said anything to her and she didn't speak either; just stared at them with a look of rage in her eyes and her pasty face speckled with splatterings of blood which gave the impression she had freckles.

After a slight hesitation, Gina made a dash forward towards Stacey who - in turn - flinched back. She didn't hit her though. She didn't even touch her. Instead, Gina reached into her pocket and pulled out the same key she had freed herself with. Still no words shared as Gina slid the key into the first lock on the chain before giving it a twist, popping it right open.

'Thank you…' Stacey said - part of her worried that this was all a cruel trick and - now she was free - she was about to be attacked. 'Thank you,' she said again.

Gina crossed the room to Mathew who held his chains out for her so that she could free him too.

'I don't know who you are but cheers,' he said as she opened his lock too.

As soon as he was able to, Mathew stood up and pulled himself free from the chain as Stacey did the same on her end of the room. Gina ran back towards the door, desperate to find her way out.

'Wait!' Mathew called out to her, stopping her in her tracks.

'Do you know the way out of here?'

Gina shook her head.

'Look - clearly we are in this mess together… I think it might be a good idea to stick together until we get out and then… Well then we can stick together or we can go our separate ways. What do you think?' Mathew continued. He looked at Stacey who nodded in agreement. A glance to Gina and it was clear she was mulling it over for a second. She too nodded and then ran from the room. Surprised by the fact she didn't wait around in order to formulate some sort of plan, Mathew and Stacey hurried after her.

* * * * *

Frank screamed at the monitor - frustrated that Gina just didn't kill everyone in the room. Despite wanting to kill Nicola himself, he was pleasantly surprised with the sheer brutality Gina had used to dispose of her but - at the same time - he knew he should have expected it. This was, after all, the woman who'd won nine out of nine fights.

Frank started frantically searching through the other available footage. Christina's attacks - and Gina's own screaming - had attracted the attention of the rest of the household and, now, the house was in complete pandemonium. A pandemonium which was about to be made worse by the fact that Gina and co. had found the cages...

'Shit's going to get interesting,' Frank laughed to himself.

If they leave the cages alone, the escapees are as good as dead. Frank knew this and - watching Gina approach the first cage - she obviously knew it too but, then, it didn't take a genius to figure that much out. After all, there were more members of the house - all busy arming themselves - then there was of Mathew, Stacey and Gina. And now the element of surprise was gone too, if the escapees did come face to face with the rest of the house, they'd be taken down within seconds - as would the few zombies already roaming around thanks to both Gina's murderous rampage and Christina's vicious bites.

'What the fuck is this place?' Mathew stuttered - his eyes fixed to the cage at the other end of the room. One cage, multiple undead within reaching their pruned fingers through the small bars.

* * * * *

Gina knew what the room was. More specifically she knew *who* the people in the cage were - or rather who they had been when they were alive. Nine people in total with the one standing at the front of the cage, closest to the door, still looking as fresh as the day she was killed.

The undead woman had been introduced to Gina as Carron Offer. The combatants were always introduced to each other before being forced to fight. A cruel act as it ensured the winner never forgot the life they took.

Carron's clouded eyes fixed onto Gina and she looked at her in such a way that Gina couldn't be sure the dead woman didn't recognise her - if only for a split second. She opened her mouth and a strained moan forced it's way up through her wind-pipe and out of her mouth with a trickle of black blood.

Mathew asked again, 'What the fuck is this room?'

Gina didn't answer him. She hurried over to the cage door; thankfully locked in a similar way to most of the other doors - a single deadbolt.

Mathew's question changed to, 'What the fuck are you doing?'

Gina looked at him. She could have spent time explaining her plan or… Avoiding the clawing fingers, she undid the lock and hurried from the room as the door slowly swung open, freeing the undead from within. Mathew and Stacey didn't hang around either.

'She's crazy!' Stacey said, hurrying through the open door back into the second floor hallway.

The trio stopped in the hallway. On one side of them, two of the undead were lurching their way down the narrow hallway with the taste for flesh on their mind, on the other side - four living members of the household; the taste for murder and revenge in their own eyes and various weapons in each of their hands.

Chad - one of the four men and the one Stacey recognised from when Frank had first introduced himself to her and Mathew - stepped forward with a baseball bat over his shoulder. He smiled directly at Stacey before pointing the tip of his bat in her direction. 'Just so you know,' he said, 'by the end of the day I am going to be balls deep inside of you. The only question is - will you be breathing at the time or will you be one of them?' he nodded towards the undead inching ever closer to the trio.

Stacey returned his smile, 'If you're going to be inside of me - I think I'd rather be dead.'

The three men standing with Chad laughed at the obvious burn.

'You fucking bitch!' Chad took a step forward with the bat back over his shoulder. 'I'll make sure I only knock you out.'

Gina turned back to the two undead. There was more chance of survival going in that direction than if she charged the four men - especially as they had weapons. At least with the dead - she just knew she had to avoid being bitten. She nudged Mathew, 'That way.'

He nodded having already had the same thought as Gina and being even more aware that the undead she had freed from the cage were getting closer to the bedroom door they'd been caged up in too.

Being bigger, Mathew led the charge back down the hallway towards the shuffling dead. Gina was right behind him with Stacey coming up the rear; the smaller of the three - she was happy to let them take the lead.

* * * * *

Frank looked down at the controls on the desk before him, seeking out a rewind button. The two zombies were on the floor, struggling to get up and Mathew, Gina and Stacey had already disappeared around the next corner and out of the screenshot. Frank didn't care about that though.

He knew he'd be able to track them when he was ready. He was more interested in seeing if what he thought he saw actually happened or whether his brain - for some reason - made it up.

No rewind button.

'Did he fucking clothes-line them?' he muttered to himself whilst silently being impressed. He hadn't seen a move like that since back in the 90s when everything was normal and his weekends was spent watching the WWE.

The answer he couldn't get confirmed, though, was "yes". Mathew - using all of his weight did clothes-line the two dead fucks; a simple, yet effective, move and one which impressed both the ladies.

'The guy's a fucking hero,' Frank laughed to himself. 'I mean - I hope he fucking dies but… Kudos for that. That was good.' He chuckled and looked back up to the screen.

Chad was on the floor by the bedroom door with the recently freed zombies. As the four housemates had gone to go past the room, the horde of the undead had come out. "Bad timing" was an understatement and yet that's exactly what it was. Carron was on top of Chad - piercing his skin with her dirty fingernails and biting his flesh - taking chunks off in large mouthfuls as he screamed. The other infected were making short work of the three men that had taken up arms alongside him.

Frank wasn't bothered. Not about that anyway. He was just desperate for a rewind button. He couldn't be sure whether Mathew had used an old WWE move and now he had missed the latest action too. It was all fun and games watching the blood spraying out of people who'd turned him into the Resident Bad-Guy and it was music to his ears to hear their screams of pain but he had wanted to see the shock on their faces as they first ran into the undead. And - just like the clothes-line - he had missed it.

'Cunts.'

CHAPTER ELEVEN

FREEDOM

The hallway led onto another hallway, and another, until finally they came back round to the front of the house and the stairs that led down towards the ground floor of the mansion.

More people had gathered in the atrium, all seemingly looking in opposite directions from each other to ensure every nook and cranny was covered and that they missed nothing; be it a surprise attack from the escapees or one of the undead. Unlike the aggressive nature of the four just encountered - they all seemed nervous.

Gina and the others stopped at the top of the stairs. The group of housemates was all that stood between them and freedom and yet they knew they wouldn't just let them walk on by. They take so much as one step down there, they'd be battered - to death, most likely.

Gina didn't wait to ask Mathew or Stacey for their thoughts on what they should do. Instead she about turned and ran up the stairs to the third - quiet at first glance - floor. Mathew and Stacey, after a final look around to see if there was a better option - followed as a newly deceased Chad appeared at the far end of the landing, coming back down from the other hallway.

'This is ridiculous,' Stacey called out as she ran up the stairs. 'How are we going to get out?'

No one answered her. Not because they didn't want to, or because they didn't hear her but because they didn't have any answers. Certainly no answer that she would have liked.

The third floor was laid out in a similar fashion to the second floor with hallways leading off to other sections of the house and a galleried landing that formed a square overlooking the ground floor.

The gathered group on the ground floor weren't chasing, despite having seen the trio. They had formed a stronghold and knew their best line of defence was to stand fast and wait for trouble to come to them. Then - and only then – would they start fighting. Not that they'd have long to wait as the undead Chad stumbled down the stairs, landing in a crumpled heap next to a young woman with a poker that she'd taken from beside the fireplace.

Before Chad's corpse had a chance to stand up, she drove the tip of the poker straight through his skull - killing him for a second, and permanent, time. Wiping a fleck of blood from her face, she yanked the poker out and readied herself for the next one of the undead fucks to land before her.

'Ironic, isn't it?' a man asked, standing next to the woman.

'What?'

'All those women he fucked and now… Well… A woman fucked him.'

The two laughed.

'Was always going to happen,' the woman said. 'Fucking creep.'

* * * * *

Mathew was looking out of the window at the end of the hallway. Third floor up. Long drop. Gina was already halfway down the next hallway, desperate for a way out. Stacey was between the two, worried that Mathew was going to get left behind or that they'd both end up losing Gina.

'Come on!' she urged him.

'Wait!' Mathew called back. He shouted louder so that Gina heard him, 'Wait!'

Gina stopped and turned to him. She almost looked annoyed that she was being held back.

Mathew ignored the pissed look on her face and continued, 'If we go down there we just know it's going to loop back round to the main stairwell… This is the best bet,' he pointed out of the window.

'What?' Stacey heard him. She just didn't believe what he was saying. 'As in - jump?'

'There's thick bushes down there,' Mathew continued pointing down to the bushes as Gina and Stacey both approached him, curious to see what he had seen. 'We can make it. The bushes will break our fall.'

'Are you fucking insane?' Stacey asked.

Gina looked out of the window. It was definitely a long drop but Mathew was right - there were bushes down there which could have broken their fall. Without a word, she grabbed a framed picture from the wall and lobbed it through the window sending shards of glass crashing below. She turned to the shocked Mathew and Stacey, 'You might want to dodge the glass,' she said, taking a step back. This was Mathew's idea. He could go first.

Mathew leaned out of the broken window. It really was a long drop. He sighed, 'Well... We stay here, we're dead anyway - right?' Grabbing another framed picture from the wall, he used the edge of it to clear away the last of the glass. When done, he tossed it to the floor. No sense throwing it out of the window and having something else to potentially land on. He glanced at the two girls and tried to look happy about what he was about to do. 'Well... See you on the ground then.'

Mathew climbed out of the window and sat there for a moment with his legs dangling outside. Looking down, his heart was beating hard and fast. He closed his eyes and then - without overthinking it - he dropped.

The air rushed past him as the ground raced upwards. He closed his eyes and tried to make his body go as limp as possible. A split second later he landed hard in the bush with a pained grunt as the wind was knocked from him. It hurt but he wasn't dead. Lying there, amongst the dirt and foliage, he couldn't help but to start laughing. Carefully, he sat up. Stacey was leaning out of the window, checking down to see if her friend was okay. He waved up to her as he rolled out of the bush.

It was her turn. Stacey had to jump, Gina had to jump and then that was it. They were free. Find a car, hit the road and don't look back. Don't come for revenge. Just move on and thank whatever God is up there that they had survived.

'I can't do it!' Stacey called down. She was sitting on the window ledge - just as Mathew had done. Her voice was shaking. 'I can't do…' Her sentence was cut-off as Gina gave her a hard shove from behind. Stacey screamed the whole way down as she plummeted into the same bush Mathew had previously landed in.

Mathew rushed to her side and dragged her from the bush after asking if she were okay.

'She fucking pushed me!' Stacey shouted. 'She fucking pushed me!'

'Relax. It's done. You're down. We're free.'

Gina landed behind them - also as safely as had been possible. Stacey immediately lashed out for her as she stumbled from the bush.

'You fucking pushed me!'

Mathew dragged her back and forced her down as a car turned onto the mansion's driveway, 'Get down!'

They didn't know who it was and they didn't care to find out as the car's headlights lit the area up as bright as daylight. They couldn't do all of this, and that jump, only to run into trouble now. Not when they were so close to their freedom.

* * * * *

Frank sat back and sighed. He was surprised that they made it. Surprised and disappointed, for sure. More so when he flicked back to the view of the main atrium. The housemates were struggling to contain the problem of the recently released (and deceased) horde spilling down the stairs. Frank could see that more people had been bitten, even though they were continuing to fight, chunks of flesh missing from their arms or necks. It was a sight which made him realise that the house he had fought to secure was all but lost. If not tonight then definitely within the next few days as the infection continued to spread.

He was safe though. All the time he was in this room, he was safe. He'd give it a couple of days and then, he'd negotiate his way out where he'd try and find somewhere else he could call home.

With the knowledge it was over, he had seen enough and leaned forward to the monitors once more. He flicked a switch and killed the power. He'd only turn it on again to check the rooms remotely before leaving. At the moment, though, it wasn't needed. It was just fucking depressing.

And yet those cunts managed to escape. Sometimes, life just isn't fair.

EPILOGUE

REBECCA and CHRIS

Chris was trying to ignore the pain in his leg as he hobbled down the road. A chain was attached to his ankle and the other end to a concrete lump which rested in the shopping trolley he pushed in front of him; a trolley that was useful for carrying the heavy weight of the boulder and for giving him support for his bad leg.

His eyes were red raw from crying after taking Rebecca's life but he was calmer now. He knew what he had to do. A walk down to the nearby lake and then he'd just stroll into it with the concrete ball in his hands. He'd keep going until he was fully submerged and out of his depth. The concrete ball had three purposes; the first being to weigh him down and stop him from changing his mind. The second purpose was for when he turned - the heavy weight of the ball would stop him from coming back out as one of *them*. The third purpose… Inside the ball, caked in quick-drying cement, was Rebecca's severed head. The concrete ball was the only burial he could afford her. He would die - drowned at the bottom of the lake - where he'd remain for eternity. Rebecca would stay by his side; together in their death.

A car horn from behind startled him. He turned just in time to see the vehicle suddenly accelerate towards him. With not enough time to dodge it, the car clipped him, killing him instantly. Inside the vehicle, Mathew laughed as he steered back into the centre of the road.

'What the fuck did you do that for?' Stacey asked.

'Remember the last time you asked me to stop and help someone?' Mathew replied casually.

'He might have been good,' she argued.

'There are no good people left anymore, Stacey. You need to get that in your head if we're going to survive.'

Stacey didn't say anything.

Gina who was sitting in the rear of the car - caked in the brains and blood of the car's original driver; the man who had pulled up onto the drive back at the house. He had climbed out of the car only to be attacked with no warning. His death dealt to him by the repeated slamming of his head between door and car. When she was done, and turned back to Mathew and Stacey - that was when Mathew said he'd drive. Give her a chance to calm down; a little time out in the back of the car.

Gina didn't argue with Mathew's point either. There were no good people left and - already in her head - she was planning on how to take the car from the two of them. Get back on the road, by herself, to try and find her family. Looking at the pair in the front of the car, she figured Mathew and Stacey would be okay. After all - they had made it this far.

They'd find another car and if they didn't? Well - fuck them.

THE END

There was another rumble from Frank's stomach. Enough was enough. Time to leave the room and find shelter and something to eat and drink. Two days was quite long enough and - besides being hungry - he was dying for the toilet, although not quite at the stage where he considered doing it in the corner of the room.

According to the screen the main parts of the house were still full of the walking dead - quietly shuffling around. Looking at the various screens, they were spaced out enough for him to hopefully be able to dodge and weave past them. It was dangerous, sure, but if he was quick…

Standing in the centre of the safe-room he stretched out his legs and eased out the stiffness caused from spending the vast majority of the last two days sat on the leather seat.

'Okay,' he muttered to himself, 'let's do this.'

He walked over to the release catch for the secret door and pressed it. Slowly the door opened. Frank froze. There, standing directly in front of him, with blood smeared around her mouth - Christina.

'Oh fuck.'

.....